'What's go[...]
been avoi[...]
why do I g[...]
suddenly w[...]
something [...]

'Something else?' he repeated, playing for time because he still wasn't sure if he was going to carry this through to the possibly *bitter* end. 'I didn't know anything had happened in the first place.'

'You know very well what I mean, so let's not split hairs. What is this all about? If it has anything to do with what happened two years ago then I think I have a right to know.'

A&E DRAMA

Blood pressure is high and pulses are racing in these fast-paced, dramatic stories from Mills & Boon® Medical Romance™. They'll move a mountain to save a life in an emergency, be they the crash team, ER doctors, fire, air and land rescue, or paramedics. There are lots of critical engagements amongst the high tensions and emotional passions in these exciting stories of lives and loves at risk!

A&E DRAMA

Hearts are racing!

RAPID RESPONSE

BY
JENNIFER TAYLOR

MILLS & BOON®

First published in Great Britain 2004
Harlequin Mills & Boon Limited,
Eton House, 18-24 Paradise Road, Richmond, Surrey TW9 1SR

© Jennifer Taylor 2004

ISBN 0 263 83917 6

Set in Times Roman 10½ on 12 pt.
03-0804-46929

Printed and bound in Spain
by Litografía Rosés, S.A., Barcelona

CHAPTER ONE

THE last time Holly Daniels had seen Ben Carlisle she'd slapped his face and told him to go to hell. That had been two years ago but she doubted if he'd forgotten what had happened any more than she had. She sighed as she tossed back her mane of chestnut curls and stood up. Oh, well, she would just have to brazen it out.

Holly crossed the room and went to join the group of people clustered around the coffee-urn. She'd met most of them already during the recent training sessions. Setting up the new rapid response team at Dalverston General Hospital had been a major undertaking and a lot of time and money had been invested in the service. The area health authority was keen to avoid any problems so the training course had been extremely tough. At least two of the candidates had dropped out and Ben had been hired to fill one of the vacancies.

'Hello, Ben.' Holly steeled herself when he swung round. It had been a shock when she'd found out yesterday that they would be working together but she had no intention of letting Ben see that it bothered her. Maybe he *had* broken her heart two years ago when he'd dumped her for another woman but she'd got over it. Eventually. Now she treated him to a cool little smile.

'How are you?'

'Holly! What are you doing here?'

'The same as you, apparently. I'm one of the specialist registrars on the team. Snap!'

It was hard to hold her smile when she saw the dismay on his face. Even though she knew it was stupid, Holly couldn't help feeling hurt. Did Ben have to make it so obvious that she was the last person he'd hoped to see?

The thought steadied her. She'd done her share of crying after they'd split up and there was no way that she would let him upset her again. Her smile widened as she looked at him with mocking green eyes.

'What's the matter, Ben? Aren't you pleased to see me?'

'I'm just surprised, that's all.' He summoned a smile but Holly could tell how shocked he was. 'I never imagined you'd leave London. You used to say that you hated the thought of leaving the bright city lights.'

'Did I?' She shrugged. 'I don't remember so I'll have to take your word for it.'

She looked round when someone banged on the table and called for order. She certainly didn't intend to admit that the reason why she'd left London had been because it had held too many memories. She and Ben had spent a lot of time exploring the city together and it had been too painful to be constantly reminded about the good times they'd had. It had been one of the reasons why she'd been so keen to take this job, in fact, because moving to Lancashire had meant a completely fresh start. How ironic that Ben should have turned up in Dalverston as well.

Holly pushed that thought out of her mind as Sean Fitzgerald, the head of Trauma Care, began his welcoming speech. He briefly outlined the set-up to make sure that everyone understood what their roles would be. The front-line team consisted of four specialist registrars and four highly trained paramedics. They would be on call to deal with any major accidents that occurred in their catchment area. Once the casualties were brought back to the hospital they would be handed over to the resus team, who were all experts in the field of trauma care. It was an exciting new venture and it was obvious that Sean was as keen to make a success of it as they all were.

'So that's it, boys and girls. I know the training has been tough and that some of you must have wondered at times what you were letting yourselves in for.' Sean grinned when a chorus of agreements greeted that remark. He held up his hand and waited until everyone was silent again.

'The work you'll be called upon to do won't be easy and you'll be expected to give one hundred and ten per cent effort. However, every single one of you has been chosen specifically for your strengths. You lot are the cream of the crop and I know that together we can make this service something really special.'

Everyone applauded loudly before the meeting broke up. There was an emergency unit to run and time was at a premium. Holly went to fetch her bag, pausing when Sean came over to speak to her. He had Ben with him and she quickly adopted a suitably neutral expression.

'I'd like you to take Ben under your wing, please, Holly. I've managed to fill him in on the basics but there hasn't been time to give him the full course of training you had.' Sean turned to Ben. 'Maybe you two could get together and swot up on any areas you're concerned about. Holly was our star pupil and I'm sure she'll be able to bring you up to speed.'

'That would be great, so long as Holly doesn't mind, of course,' Ben said quietly, but Holly could hear the reservation in his voice even if Sean had missed it.

Her mouth compressed as she picked up her bulging tote bag. Did Ben hate the thought of having her act as his tutor because he felt guilty about what he'd done two years ago? Or was she kidding herself by thinking that he cared a jot?

Probably the latter, she decided, tucking the bag under her arm. If Ben had possessed even an ounce of decency then he would never have treated her the way he had.

'Holly?'

She looked up when she realised that Sean was waiting for her to confirm that she was happy about his suggestion. Even though helping Ben was the last thing she felt like doing, she couldn't admit that. It had been drummed into them during the training sessions that they were all part of a team and that it was only by working as a team that they would make a success of this venture. How could she blot her copy book at such an early stage by refusing to help a colleague?

'I'll be pleased to help any way I can,' she said with a sweet smile that didn't fool Ben for a second if his expression was anything to go by. Thankfully, Sean seemed oblivious to the undercurrents as he beamed at them both.

'Great! That's a weight off my mind. Having to find a last-minute replacement has been a real headache. I had some sleepless nights until I heard that Ben was interested in the job.' He clapped the younger man on the shoulder. 'I know you've had it rough in the last few years but let's hope this is a turning point for you. We need doctors of your calibre.'

Holly frowned. She had no idea what Sean had meant about Ben having had a rough time. She looked enquiringly at him when Sean moved away. 'That sounded intriguing. What's been happening to you of late, then?'

'Oh, nothing very interesting.' Ben briskly changed the subject. 'Look, Holly, I know how…well… *awkward* this must be for you….'

'Awkward?' She felt herself bridling and glared at him, unable to believe the arrogance of that statement. 'Why should *I* feel the least bit awkward?'

'Because we didn't exactly part on the best of terms, if you recall.' His expression darkened as he returned her look with one which held more than a hint of challenge. 'You aren't going to pretend that you've forgotten what happened, I hope. That's nonsense, as well you know.'

'Of course I haven't forgotten!' She laughed scornfully, enjoying the fact that he seemed so rattled. Good! He deserved his comeuppance after the appalling way he'd treated her. 'What you did to me, Ben, was such a rotten, low-down thing to do to anyone that there's no way I'll ever forget it.'

'I know how it must have seemed,' he began, but she carried on, cutting off his apology if, indeed, an apology was what he'd intended.

'But in a way I'm grateful to you for what you did.'

'Grateful?'

The surprise in his voice was like balm to her soul and went a long way towards making up for all those nights she'd spent, sobbing into her pillow. She smiled at him, seeing the shock that had turned his blue eyes the colour of a stormy sky. Ben had always been sinfully handsome and she, like so many women, had fallen for his dark good looks. However, she felt nothing when she looked at him now, she assured herself, not even a flicker of interest. She was well and truly over him and her heart was once more whole again even if there were scars on it.

'Yes. You taught me a valuable lesson, Ben, made me see how stupid it is to rely on anyone else for your happiness. You have to take charge of your life and do what *you* want.' She shrugged. 'That's why I'm grateful to you because I'll never make the same mistake again. I'm my own woman now, Ben, not someone's girlfriend or lover. And d'you know what? It feels good to be me!'

*   *   *

Ben wished he could believe that but there was no way he could ignore the underlying pain in Holly's voice. It was proof of how much he'd hurt her two years ago and there was no way he could make amends for what he'd done. He couldn't tell her the truth, couldn't admit that there had been no other woman, because it would lead to questions he wasn't prepared to answer.

Finding out two years ago that he had cancer of the colon had rocked his whole world. All he'd been able to think about had been that he mustn't let it affect Holly in any way. He'd seen the devastating effects that dealing with serious illness could have and had sworn he wouldn't put Holly through that ordeal. She'd been just starting out on her career with her whole future ahead of her and it wouldn't have been fair to burden her with his problems. So he'd made the decision not to tell her and had made up some story about meeting someone else.

Lying to her had been the hardest thing he'd ever done but it had been the right decision. Holly had been able to get on with her life and that was what he'd wanted so desperately. Now he had to make sure she never found out the truth because it would only cause problems. He had to forget the past and focus on the present, although it wasn't going to be easy. Working with Holly would be a constant reminder of what he'd lost.

'Then all I can say is that I'm glad you're happy.' He smiled, aiming for nonchalance and probably missing it by miles. 'I'd hate there to be any problems about us working together.'

'No chance of that, I assure you.'

She laughed and Ben felt his stomach muscles bunch when his mind immediately logged the sound and found a matching one in his memory bank. Holly's laughter had been the very first thing he'd noticed about her and it was hard not to remember what had happened that day, how he had stopped on his way through Casualty when he'd heard her laughing then had turned around to go back and find her.

Memories whizzed around inside his head and he winced because it was painful to think about the past when he'd been determined to forget it. Holly had been attending to a small boy when he'd tracked her down and he could still remember how glorious her chestnut curls had looked as they'd tumbled around her face when she'd bent to hug the child. He must have made some sort of sound because she'd suddenly looked round and it had felt as though he'd been hit by a sledgehammer when he'd got his first glimpse of her face. He'd never believed that love at first sight had existed outside the pages of a romance novel until that moment...

'Ben?'

Holly tapped him on the arm, rather hard and definitely impatiently, and he jumped. 'What?'

'We've got our first shout. Didn't you hear what Sean said?'

She didn't bother waiting for him to answer as she hurried to the door. Ben followed in her wake, delighted to have something to shift his brain out of its introspective mode. It was the present that mattered, he reminded himself, what was happening at this very minute, and already he could feel the excitement building as everyone gathered in the office.

'RTA on the road leading through Dalverston Fell,' Sean announced. 'A coach full of tourists has overturned. There's a five-mile tailback of traffic so we'll be using the helicopter and the motorbike for speed. Holly, you take the bike. The police have given us a map reference so use the satellite navigation system to find a route that will avoid the traffic.'

Ben moved aside as Holly stepped forward and took the details from Sean. She didn't look at him as she hurried from the room so he didn't have a chance to tell her to be careful. He sighed because he could just imagine her reaction if he had. Holly had made it plain that she didn't need his input into her life and he must remember that.

Fortunately, there was no time to dwell on that depressing thought because Sean was rattling out instructions. Ben nodded when he was informed that he was one of the staff who would be going in the helicopter. He followed the others out of the office and collected his flight-suit then made his way to the helipad on the roof of the hospital. Nicky Brunswick and Josh Hammond, the two paramedics, were joking about it being just their luck not to have had time for a second cup of coffee but Ben could tell they were as excited as he was. This was their first real test as a team and they needed to prove that all the money that had been invested in the service hadn't been wasted.

The take-off was remarkably smooth so that within

seconds they were circling the hospital. Ben stared out of the helicopter window, watching the ground rushing past below. He caught a glimpse of something green and white turning out of the hospital's gates and felt his pulse leap when he realised it was Holly on the motorbike. He watched until she disappeared from sight then sat back and tried to compose himself. An incident like this could present many problems and he would have to deal with whatever came his way. Still, he had plenty of back-up because Nicky and Josh would be there to help, plus Holly, of course.

His mind latched onto her name and wouldn't seem to let it go again. Ben felt the fluttering of excitement build into a steady hum and knew it wasn't solely because of what he might be called upon to do. That would be taxing enough but it was the thought of working with Holly that was making his nerves twang like rusty guitar strings.

Could he remain impartial around her? He hoped so. He really did. But he couldn't put his hand on his heart and swear that the past wouldn't intrude at some point.

Holly could feel her tension mounting as she neared the site of the accident. The satellite navigation system had made a huge difference by helping her find a route that had avoided the worst of the traffic. The fact that the motorbike could slip through gaps a car couldn't pass through meant that she should arrive well before any ambulances got there. There was only the helicopter that could beat her and even that would need to find a place to land. She might be the first medic on scene and she had to prepare herself for what she was going to find.

She rounded the final bend and skidded to a halt when she spotted the coach up ahead. It was lying on its side and even from that distance she could tell it was very badly damaged. Part of the roof had sheared off when it had rolled down the banking and there was broken glass and lumps of metal strewn across the nearby fields. There were also a few people wandering about so she hastily put the motorbike into gear and rode straight over to the young police officer who had been first on the scene and removed her helmet so she could introduce herself.

'I'm Holly Daniels, specialist reg from Dalverston General.'

'They're sending someone else as well, I hope,' the policeman said anxiously. He was obviously deeply shocked by the scale of the accident and Holly uttered a silent prayer that someone with more experience would be sent to take charge. Dealing with an accident of this magnitude required a great deal of skill. Although the emergency services worked closely together—fire, police and ambulance crews each playing a vital role—it needed someone with experience to bring it all together.

'There's a helicopter on its way and a fleet of ambulances should be here very shortly,' she assured him, taking her Thomas pack—the bag of vital medical supplies that she carried—out of the pannier. She looked up when the sound of an engine confirmed the arrival of the helicopter. 'Here's the 'copter now, in fact. See if you can help the pilot find a safe place to land.'

She left the policeman to deal with the helicopter and ran towards the coach. There were two bodies lying on the grass and a quick check soon established there was nothing she could do for them. A woman came staggering towards her with blood streaming down her face, and Holly quickly grabbed hold of her arm.

'Sit down.' She made the woman sit on the banking then took a wad of lint out of her bag and placed it over the gash on her forehead. 'Hold this there and keep some pressure on it to stop the bleeding.'

The woman didn't say a word but she did as she was told so Holly left her. The rules were quite simple in this type of situation: the walking wounded should be given minimal treatment so that time could be spent on the severely injured. It might appear heartless but she couldn't afford to waste precious time attending to someone who really didn't need her help. There was an elderly couple huddled together nearby so she ran over to them next.

'Are you hurt?'

'My arm…' The old lady showed her a blue-veined arm and Holly winced when she saw that the bone was protruding through the flesh.

'That looks nasty.' She took a dressing out of her bag and gently placed it over the wound to minimise the risk of infection. 'Try to keep your arm very still. I know it must be terribly painful but there isn't much I can do for you here, I'm afraid. You'll be taken to hospital as soon as the ambulances arrive. Is there anything else wrong with either of you?'

'No, no,' the old man assured her. 'We're fine. It's the people in the coach who need your help, dear.'

'I'll do all I can for them,' Holly assured him as she stood up. 'You just stay there and someone will be with you very shortly.'

She ran straight over to the coach but it was impossible to see inside it because it was lying on its side. She tossed her bag onto the chassis then scrambled up after it and carefully made her way to one of the windows. She could hear people calling for help but it was difficult to tell how many were trapped inside the vehicle.

'So what have we got?'

Suddenly Ben was there and Holly felt her heart leap when she swung round and discovered how close he was. He was kneeling right beside her and it would have taken very little to tuck her hand into his and lay her head on his shoulder…

She recoiled in horror and saw his expression darken but there was nothing she could do about it. An hour ago she'd claimed to be immune to him and it hadn't been an idle claim either. She'd spent months shoring up her emotions and hardening her heart against the memories because it hadn't been her fault that they'd split up but his. He had fallen in love with someone else so there'd been no point dwelling on the good times they'd had. She had torn up the photographs, thrown away all the silly little notes he'd been in the habit of leaving around the flat for her to find and had erased every trace of Ben Carlisle from her life.

She'd done a good job, too, because she hadn't thought about him for—oh, at least two months. She had been confident that Ben was out of her system but if that was true, why had she responded to him just now? Why had she longed to touch him, lean against him, snuggle into his arms and play the loving little woman when it had got her absolutely nowhere first time around? Was she so pathetic that she needed to have the message hammered home to her again?

Ben never loved you. He just used you. You were a convenience to him, good in bed and more than willing to provide him with sex!

'Damn it, Holly, don't *do* that!'

Holly jumped. 'Do what?' she muttered, struggling to rid her mind of that taunting little voice.

'Look at me as though I'm some kind of…of ogre!' He glowered at her. 'Working with you is going to be a nightmare if you insist on walking round with that massive chip on your shoulder. What happened between us is history and it's about time you got over it!'

CHAPTER TWO

BEN couldn't remember another time when he'd felt like such a louse. Apart from when he'd told Holly that lie, of course, and 'louse' wasn't the word he would have used to describe himself then. He held his breath as he watched myriad expressions cross her face before she finally settled on anger. Good! He could put up with anything she cared to dish out so long as he didn't have to see her looking so stricken.

'Don't flatter yourself, Ben Carlisle! I got over you a long time ago and there's no chip on my shoulder, I assure you.'

'Then let's get on with what we're here for.'

Ben crouched down and peered inside the coach. He could feel the waves of antipathy emanating from her but steadfastly ignored them. It was neither the time nor the place to deal with this issue because, despite what Holly had said, there definitely was an issue. Holly had been deeply hurt by the way he'd behaved two years ago and it was still having an effect on her. If he did nothing else then he would have to find a way to set her free so that she could move on.

The thought of exactly *how* Holly might choose to do that was unsettling. Even though Ben knew that he'd forfeited any rights where she was concerned,

he hated the thought of her being involved with another man. Fortunately for him, the present situation
was too grim to allow him to worry about it so he
put it out of his mind while he focused on the problem of finding a way inside the coach. One of the
windows further along from where they were kneeling had shattered during the crash so he pointed towards it.

'I need to get inside so let's try over there.'

Holly stood up then had to grab hold of his shoulder and steady herself when the coach started to rock.
The vehicle had stopped before it had reached the
bottom of the embankment and there was a very real
danger that it could start moving again if they
weren't careful.

'Take your time,' Ben instructed. 'If this thing
rolls over then we'll go with it. I don't fancy being
squashed flat under several tons of metal.'

'I don't suppose the passengers who are stuck inside fancy it either,' she shot back, obviously still
furious with him.

'I'm sure they don't,' he replied mildly to defuse
the situation. Holly had a fiery temper and he didn't
want to run the risk of her getting hurt because she
wasn't thinking clearly. 'So let's take it nice and
steady for all our sakes.'

She shot him a smouldering look but, nevertheless,
did as he'd suggested. Ben breathed a sigh of relief
when she crouched down and began to inch her way
forwards on her hands and knees. However, his relief
was short-lived because from this angle he suddenly

realised that he had a perfect view of her pert little bottom.

He ground his teeth as a surge of purely male appreciation swept through him. Holly is just a colleague doing a job, he reminded himself sternly as he followed her along the coach. He must focus on that instead of letting himself get carried away by how attractive that lurid shade of green could look in the right circumstances. Holly was wearing one of the regulation uniforms that had been issued to all the members of the rapid response team. It was similar in style to his own flight-suit and had knee pads and umpteen zippered pockets. Nobody would have classed the garment as *sexy* but, then, few people had been privy to the view he was currently enjoying. Holly's taut little derrière did wonders for the baggy garment!

It was a huge comfort when they reached their destination at last and Ben could concentrate exclusively on the problem of getting inside the coach. He peered through the window then turned to Holly. 'I should be able to get through there with a bit of luck. Can you pass me the bag once I'm down?'

'OK.'

She didn't waste time by asking questions, just moved aside to give him room to lower himself through the opening. It was a bit of a squeeze because his flight-suit was extremely bulky but he knew better than to take it off. The fabric it was made from had a twenty-second fire resistancy and that could be vital to his safety.

Holly lowered the Thomas pack down to him then

swung her legs through the opening. Ben shook his head when he realised that she intended to climb down into the coach as well. 'I can manage. It's a real mess in here so you stay up there.'

She ignored him as she wriggled through the window and lowered herself into the coach. Ben glared at her. 'Didn't you hear what I said?'

'Yes, I heard. And when Sean tells me that you're in charge then I'll do as you say. Until then I'll make up my own mind about what needs doing, thank you very much.'

She squeezed past him and went to check on an elderly woman who was lying by the door. Ben swore under his breath but he knew she'd made a valid point. He had no right to issue orders or expect her to carry out his wishes. Two years ago he'd been her boss although he would never have dreamt of pulling rank. It had been such a pleasure to teach her and watch her growing increasingly confident. However, the time he'd had to take out of his career while he'd undergone treatment for his illness had set him back and he had to remember they were on an equal footing now.

It was another adjustment he would need to make in the coming weeks and it wasn't going to be easy, but he had to forget about their past relationship and concentrate on the demands of this job. Gaining back some of the ground he'd lost was important to him and he wasn't going to let anything stop him. He glanced at Holly and his mouth compressed. If Holly could handle this situation then, by heaven, so could he.

*   *   *

'I can't find a pulse.' Holly frowned as she pressed her fingers against the artery in the driver's right ankle. She waited a moment then shook her head. 'No, still nothing.'

'We're going to have to get him out of there,' Ben replied curtly. 'He'll lose that leg if we can't restore the circulation pretty soon.'

'See if you can get one of the fire crew to cut him out,' she suggested, pushing the hair out of her eyes with a grubby forearm. Her hands, encased in a double layer of gloves, were covered in blood and there was more blood soaking through the knees of her uniform. The driver had been trapped in his seat by the steering column, which had buckled during the impact. He'd suffered a serious injury to his right thigh and had lost a lot of blood. They had rigged up a drip but as fast as they were pumping fluid into him, more blood was gushing out. Holly reapplied pressure to stem the flow but she knew the driver wouldn't survive if he wasn't freed soon.

'I'll see what I can do.'

Ben got up and scrambled over the tangle of metal that had once comprised the first few rows of seats. One of the firemen was using an oxyacetylene torch to free a young woman who was trapped in the third row and the noise was deafening. They had managed to get most of the injured out now so there was just the driver and the girl left. She looked up when Ben came back and her heart sank when he shook his head.

'No go. They daren't use any more cutting gear in

here because of the risk of fire. Apparently, the fuel tank is full and the build-up of heat could ignite it.'

'Great! We'll just have to keep our fingers crossed that they get that girl out soon so they can start on the driver next.'

Holly looked round when she saw Nicky Brunswick making her way towards them. Nicky had been monitoring the young woman and Holly grimaced when she saw the worried expression on the paramedic's face. 'Don't tell me—more problems?'

'Looks like it.' Nicky rolled her eyes. 'It only turns out that she's seven months pregnant and her waters have just broken.'

'Oh, that's just what we need!' Holly exclaimed. 'How long will it be before they manage to free her, d'you know?'

'Another five minutes or so,' Nicky began, then groaned when a scream rang around the coach. 'Oh, please, don't let that be the baby arriving already!'

'You take over here while I go and see what's happening,' Holly instructed. 'You'll need to maintain pressure to control the bleeding.'

'It doesn't look as though he's got that much blood left to lose,' Nicky observed darkly. 'It's like an abattoir round here.'

'And how would you know what an abattoir looks like?' Holly demanded as they swopped places. She and Nicky had become good friends during the training sessions. They'd got on so well, in fact, that they'd decided to share a flat. Now she grinned at her friend. 'I don't know who you've been dating recently but a visit to the local abattoir certainly isn't my idea of a fun night out.'

'Depends on who you go with,' Nicky replied archly.

'The man hasn't been born who could get me to a place like that,' Holly retorted. 'I expect a lot more than that from anyone who hopes to take me out on a date.'

'So that's your secret, is it? Treat 'em mean and keep 'em keen?' Nicky laughed. 'It certainly seems to work if Josh is anything to go by. The poor guy is totally besotted. I've heard nothing but *Holly this* and *Holly that* ever since you two met. It will be wedding bells soon if I'm not mistaken.'

'Rubbish! Josh is just a friend,' Holly replied tartly. It was complete nonsense, of course, although she couldn't stop herself glancing at Ben to see how he'd reacted to the comment before it struck her what she was doing.

She turned away, praying that he hadn't noticed. It was none of Ben's business what she did! She was a free agent and could go out with a dozen different men if that was what she chose to do. She didn't need his permission or his blessing. Ben had made his choice two years ago and he hadn't chosen *her*.

It was sobering to realise the effect that decision had had on her life. As she made her way down the coach, Holly found herself thinking that Nicky was right in a way. Her attitude towards men had hardened in the past two years. When she'd been with Ben she'd been perfectly happy to fall in with his wishes and had tailored her life to fit in with his, but she didn't make that mistake nowadays. This was *her* life and she intended to live it *her* way, and if that sounded selfish, she wasn't going to apologise for it…

But was she *really* happy? a small voice whispered. Could she honestly claim that she didn't feel as though she was missing out by adopting such a hard-nosed attitude? Didn't she sometimes long to be in a relationship again where the other person's needs were more important than her own?

Holly took a deep breath. She'd made up her mind how she intended to live her life and she was going to stick to it. She went straight to the young woman and crouched down beside her. The noise from the oxyacetylene cutter was tremendous and Holly could well appreciate why the poor soul looked so scared.

'I'm Holly Daniels and I'm a doctor at Dalverston General Hospital,' she shouted above the roaring. 'Can you tell me your name?'

'Charity Adams.'

'So, Charity, Nicky tells me that your waters have broken. Is that right?'

'Yes. I'm only seven months pregnant, too, so the baby shouldn't be born for ages…' Charity stopped talking and groaned. 'Oh, that hurts!'

Holly grimaced. 'It sounds as though you're in labour but I'll need to take a look at you before I can be sure.'

She stood up and quickly explained to the firemen that she needed to examine the girl. They turned off the torch and tactfully moved aside while she removed the protective blanket that had been placed over Charity and helped her out of her underwear. Her heart sank when she saw that the woman's cervix was fully dilated because it meant the birth was imminent.

'How long will it take to free her?' Holly asked one of the firemen.

'Just a couple more minutes.'

'Then let's get on with it. We need to get her out of here as fast as we can.'

Holly looked round when Ben came to join her. She drew him aside so that Charity couldn't hear what she was saying. 'The baby's on its way. I'm hoping we have time to get her out of here before it arrives but it's going to be a close call from the look of her. She's fully dilated.'

'I'll tell the ambulance to stand by. I'm just going to organise a stretcher, ready for when they cut the driver free. We don't want any more hold-ups.'

'Good idea,' Holly agreed. She frowned as he moved away because she couldn't help noticing how grim he looked. Obviously, the situation with the driver in particular was extremely worrying but she had a feeling it wasn't that which was bothering Ben most of all. Had it been that reference to her and Josh perhaps?

Charity gave another loud groan and Holly put that foolish thought out of her head. Ben had had his chance so why should he care if there was a legion of men interested in her?

The girl was in a great deal of pain but it was far too risky to administer pain relief at this stage when the baby was so premature. The normal analgesics used during childbirth could cause respiratory problems in pre-term babies. Whilst it might be acceptable to use them in the safety of a well-equipped maternity unit, they didn't have that luxury here. She would have to rely on talking Charity through the birth.

'Try to work with the pain and don't fight it,' she advised, taking hold of the girl's hand and giving it a reassuring squeeze. 'I want you to try and breathe nice and slowly—big deep breaths in through your nose and out through your mouth… That's it. You're doing great.'

Holly looked up when the fireman tapped her on the shoulder and told her they were ready to remove the seat. Ben came back just then and between them they managed to help Charity out of the gap. They had to stop when another contraction began but as soon as it was over, they set about getting her out of the coach. A ladder had been set up through one of the windows but Charity stopped dead and refused to carry on when she realised that she was going to have to climb up it.

'I can't get up there!' she wailed. 'What if the baby comes?'

'Holly will be right behind you.' Ben put a comforting arm around her shoulders. 'She won't let you fall and she certainly won't let anything happen to your baby.'

'But it's almost here. I can tell!' The girl clung grimly to the metal rungs, shaking her head when

Ben tried once more to urge her up the ladder. 'No! I can't do it and you can't make me!'

'Maybe we can deliver the baby here,' Holly began, but Ben didn't let her finish.

'That isn't an option.'

He took hold of Charity's hands, ignoring Holly as he set about persuading the girl to do what he wanted. Holly didn't say anything but she was seething with anger at his high-handed attitude. Ben seemed to think that he could boss her around but he was mistaken if he thought she was going to meekly do his bidding. As she'd told him once already that day, he was no longer her boss.

A frown puckered her brow as that thought sank in. Ben had been two years ahead of her when they'd met—he'd already been a registrar when she'd been a lowly houseman. He had been extremely good at his job and had had a promising future ahead of him, too. That being the case, what was he doing at Dalverston? He should have been a consultant by now, not a specialist registrar, and been on his way towards a post as head of department. So what had gone wrong? Why had his career apparently come to a standstill in the last two years? And why did she have a feeling that the answers to those questions were important?

'Are you ready, Holly? We need to get a move on.'

Holly blinked when Ben spoke to her. He'd somehow managed to convince Charity that she must climb the ladder because the girl had her foot on the first rung. Even though Holly was desperate to find out more about his career, it really wasn't the right time to ask questions. She went to join them, shaking her head when Charity had another change of heart and stepped down.

'You can do this, Charity. There's just a dozen rungs to climb then you and your baby will be safe.'

Charity took a shuddering breath and placed her foot back on the rung. 'I can do this,' she muttered. 'I can climb up this ladder.'

'Be careful, won't you?'

Ben touched her on the arm and Holly felt her heart leap when she saw the concern in his eyes. How many times had she seen him looking at her that very same way? she thought wonderingly.

'Josh is up top and I'm sure he's only too *eager* to give you a helping hand but don't rush. We don't need any more problems to contend with at the moment.'

The acerbic note in his voice when he mentioned the paramedic might have gone unnoticed by most people but not by her. No way. Holly bristled with resentment. 'And what's that supposed to mean? Do you have a problem with me and Josh?'

'Not at all.' His smile made a mockery of what she'd been thinking earlier. She didn't need to hear the indifference in his voice to know that she'd been mad to imagine Ben still cared about her. He never really had cared, if the truth be told, and the proof of that was the way he had dumped her so callously. It was an effort to hide her hurt when he continued.

'As you pointed out, Holly, it's not my place to comment on what you do.'

'No, it isn't. I'm glad you realise that.'

She didn't say anything else because there wasn't time. Charity had moved up another rung and Holly quickly followed. They had to stop when another contraction began but it wasn't long before they were able to carry on. However, it was a relief when they reached the top of the ladder where there were people waiting to help the young mother the rest of the way.

Josh grabbed hold of Holly's arm when she scrambled out onto the side of the coach and stood there, blinking. It seemed so bright outside after the gloom inside the coach that she couldn't focus for a moment.

'Are you OK, Holly?'

The concern in the handsome young paramedic's voice was wonderfully soothing after her recent spat with Ben and she smiled warmly. 'I'm fine now, thank you very much.'

'Good!' Josh gave her a quick hug then went to supervise as Charity was helped down to the ground. A plastic chute had been set up against the coach and Charity was able to slide down it without too much difficulty.

Holly sighed as she watched Josh helping the girl to a waiting ambulance. Had her response had been a bit *too* warm just now? She didn't want to give Josh the wrong idea, especially not when it might upset Ben…

'Damn, damn, damn!'

The curses sprang from her lips when she realised what she was doing again. Even after everything that had happened, she was *still* considering Ben's feelings! She swung round when she heard someone laugh and saw Nicky climbing out of the coach.

'Tut, tut, is that *really* the kind of language a well brought-up young lady should use?' Nicky grinned at her. 'If I didn't know better, I'd say you had man trouble, Holly Daniels.'

'Not a chance,' Holly retorted. 'I've too much sense to let any man cause me grief.'

Nicky whistled in admiration. 'I wish I had your attitude. I keep telling myself that I need to toughen up but I'm such a marshmallow when it comes to affairs of the heart. I envy you, Hol, really I do, although I hope poor Josh realises what he's letting himself in for.'

'I wouldn't dream of *deliberately* hurting Josh, or anyone else for that matter,' Holly denied in dismay.

'Oh, I know that! And I didn't mean to imply that you would. It's just that you have your life all worked out and refuse to be messed about.' Nicky smiled placatingly. 'I'm hoping to learn a lot from you while we're flat-sharing. If I can get my act together like you've done, Holly, then I'll be a happy bunny!'

Holly sighed as Nicky disappeared down the chute. Nicky seemed to think that her life was perfect but it was a long way away from being that. She may have achieved a certain stability recently but that could change now Ben was back on the scene. She might claim to be over him but if that was true, why did she feel so on edge? Was it possible that she still felt something for him?

She glanced round as another paramedic appeared

with a stretcher that would be used to move the driver, suddenly glad that she didn't have the time to answer that question right then. She quickly made her way back inside the coach and discovered that the fire crew had finally freed the driver. Between them they managed to shift him onto the stretcher. However, getting him out of the coach proved to be a major task. The stretcher had to be hauled out through the window with the aid of ropes and it was a worrying time for everyone concerned.

Ben heaved a sigh of relief as they watched the ambulance roar away with its sirens wailing. He looked almost as exhausted as she felt but there was a gleam in his eyes that she'd seen many times before, a light that sprang from satisfaction at a job well done. Her heart knocked against her ribs because she didn't want to think about the past right then.

'That seems to be it, then. Everyone accounted for so it's back to base now, I think.'

'Sounds like a good idea to me.' She treated him to a brief smile then quickly made her way back to where she'd left the motorbike. She wasn't going to fall into the trap again. The past was the past and she refused to keep harping on about it all the time. She *had* got over Ben—*ages* ago! The only way he could gain any power over her now was if she let him back into her life and that simply wasn't going to happen. To put it bluntly, Ben Carlisle was history!

CHAPTER THREE

'EVER had the feeling that someone must have spread the word that we were open for business today?'

'It has been pretty hectic,' Ben agreed ruefully as he followed Sean into the office.

It was the end of his shift and he'd been going off duty when Sean had asked to speak to him. The day had been one of the busiest Ben could remember. The coach crash had been followed by another RTA, this time in the town centre. Once again the resulting tailback of traffic had caused problems for the ambulance crews so he'd been asked to attend on the motorbike. Fortunately, nobody had sustained any really serious injuries that time but he'd only just got back to the hospital when another call had come in to go to a nursing home on the outskirts of Dalverston. One of the kitchen staff had been badly burnt when a fat fryer had caught fire and it had soon become apparent that the woman would need transferring to the specialist burns unit at Manchester.

He and Holly had travelled in the helicopter together because of the seriousness of the patient's condition. They'd been far too busy stabilising the woman on the outward journey to make conversation and Holly had opted to sit next to the pilot on the way back. Nothing had been said but Ben suspected that she'd been keeping her distance from him and really couldn't blame her. He'd had no right to use *that* tone when he'd spoken about Josh Hammond that morning.

The thought made him sigh and he saw Sean glance at him. 'Problems?'

'Just the usual ones, like the fact that I'm absolutely bushed and can't face the thought of cooking myself a meal when I get in. Looks like it will be a take-away again tonight,' he replied, making a note to be on his guard in future. He had to keep this problem with Holly under wraps so it wouldn't cause any disruptions within the team. It was up to them to sort things out, although the thought of having to confront her wasn't a pleasant one. He was more than happy to put it aside when Sean laughed.

'Been there, done that and had the indigestion to prove it!' Sean replied, sitting down behind the desk. 'What you need is a good woman to take you in hand, my friend.'

'Pass!' Ben grimaced as he pulled up a chair. 'I'd rather put up with the indigestion and save myself a whole load of problems, thank you very much.'

Sean shook his head. 'You don't know what you're missing. Life has been fantastic since Claire and I got married. I don't know how I ever managed without her and the kids, in fact.'

'Then you're one of the lucky ones,' Ben said lightly.

'Oh, I know that.' Sean chuckled. 'And I also know that sounds horribly smug but I'm not going to apologise for it. Anyway, enough of my eulogising about my good fortune. What I wanted to know was if there were any areas you felt I might be able help you with. And before you ask, no, I don't have any concerns about your ability to do the job. You missed the extra training the rest of the team received and I just want to make sure that you're happy with everything that's happened so far.'

'Everything has been fine today, although there might be times when I'll need a helping hand,' Ben said honestly. 'I made up a lot of the time I'd lost while I was working with Heather Cooper at St Gertrude's. She encouraged me to sit the Royal College of Physicians exams once I decided to specialise in accident and emergency medicine. I was actually thinking about applying to do a stint at HEMS when Heather told me about this new unit you'd set up here.'

'I based a lot of it on the HEMS system,' Sean explained. 'London's Helicopter Emergency Service is second to none and they gave me a lot good advice. Obviously, we're working in a rural area rather than a city but the same principles apply. Time is of the essence if you want to save lives.' He broke off and smiled. 'Hi, what can I do for you?'

Ben felt his pulse jerk when he glanced round and saw Holly standing in the doorway. She'd changed out of her working clothes and the sight of her slender body clad in a simple denim skirt and a T-shirt sent a rush of heat through his veins. She'd pinned her thick chestnut hair into a knot on the top of her head but tiny wisps were already escaping and curling about her ears. She looked so young and lovely that he wanted to drink in her beauty and let it soak away the stresses of the day but he didn't dare indulge in such pleasures unless he was willing to risk making a fool of himself.

He turned back to the desk, his heart pounding when Holly came and stood behind his chair. He could smell the faint aroma of antiseptic that clung to her skin—a scent they probably all carried on them—yet on Holly it smelled so seductive that his body immediately quickened. Ben stifled a groan, praying that Holly couldn't tell what was happening. If she ever found out that the smell of antiseptic had caused him to have an erection, she'd think he was perverted!

'Sorry to interrupt you, Sean, but I thought you'd like to know that the coach driver is out of Theatre. There's a good chance he won't lose his leg, too,' she said, steadfastly ignoring Ben as she addressed Sean over the top of his head.

'That's wonderful! I know the prognosis wasn't great when Max first saw him,' Sean declared, referring to Max Jenkins, the head of the trauma surgery team. 'But obviously things have worked out better than we feared. I don't know if you've heard but Charity Adams had a baby girl. She's been taken to the prem baby unit but they're not expecting any major problems apparently, so that's another success you two can notch up. Obviously, you make a great team.'

'I'm sure the outcome would have been the same no matter who'd treated them,' Holly said quietly, but Ben knew that what she was really trying to say

was that she didn't think their alliance had been anything special.

Was she worried in case Sean decided to team
them up again in the future? he thought with a flash
of bitterness. So far as Holly was concerned, he could
take a long walk off a short pier and it was upsetting
to realise how much she disliked him.

'Maybe, but some people just seem to have a nat-
ural affinity and work well together. I'll certainly
bear it in mind,' Sean stated, oblivious to the problems he might be creating.

Ben was hard-pressed to conceal his dismay.
Being constantly paired up together would be a rec-
ipe for disaster if they didn't manage to resolve their
differences. When Holly turned to leave, he stood up
because something needed to be done about the situation.

'If that's all, Sean, I'll see if Holly can spare me
a few minutes to go over a couple of things,' he
explained, ignoring the hostile look she shot his way
as he followed her to the door.

'Good idea, but don't work too hard. Don't forget
that you've got to come back here tomorrow and do
this all over again!'

'We won't.' Ben's jaw was aching from the effort
of keeping his smile tacked into place. Holly was
sending some very nasty vibes his way and he could
tell that she was furious with him. He closed the
office door then took her by the arm and propelled
her along the corridor, looking for somewhere that
would afford them some privacy. Resus was empty

so he steered her in there and made sure the door
was shut before he released her.

'Who the hell do you think you are, manhandling
me like that?' she snarled like a small cat that had
been backed into a corner.

'I'm sorry but it was the only way to stop you
saying something stupid,' he shot back with a sad
lack of tact.

'Don't you dare call me stupid.'

'I'm sorry! OK?' He took a deep breath and
counted to ten when he realised he'd shouted back
at her. Nobody had ever been able to rile him the
way Holly could. She'd always possessed the ability
to make him respond to her whether it was in anger
or in passion.

His brain captured that last word and ran away
with it. Ben's heart raced as he suddenly recalled
how it had been between them in the past, how easily
their passion for each other had been roused. All he'd
had to do had been to touch her—just the lightest,
most *delicate* of touches, too—and sparks had ig-
nited. They used to joke about it, in fact, one of those
silly jokes that lovers shared about lighting the blue
touch paper and standing back, and the memory
brought a rush of tears to his eyes.

How he *ached* to relive the passion they had once
shared, to run his hands over her skin and watch her
body coming to life, feel *her* hands caressing *him*
and making him feel whole again. Holly could make
him feel as he'd used to feel, like someone who
didn't need to be afraid of what the future held. She
could give him back his life and the thought filled

him with despair because there was no way that he could let her do that for him. Even though his consultant had told him the prognosis was good, there was no *guarantee* that his cancer wouldn't return. He could never get involved with Holly again because he wouldn't take the risk of breaking her heart a second time.

'Ben, what's the matter? Ben!'

Holly could feel a lump of fear in the pit of her stomach. Ben didn't say a word and the sight of him standing there with tears in his eyes was more than she could bear. She put her arms around him and hugged him because there was no other way she could think of that might help. Ben had always been so strong in the past and to see him looking so afraid now almost broke her heart.

'It's OK,' she murmured, reaching up to stroke his hair. Ben had always worn his hair short but it was shorter than ever now, she realised in surprise, and the texture felt different, too, far less silky and a lot coarser than it had been.

Oddly unsettled by the discovery, she let her hands move down to his shoulders and was alarmed to discover how bony they felt. He was still wearing his flight-suit but not even the bulky clothing could disguise his thinness. She could feel his hip bones jutting into her, feel the hard sinews in his thighs pressing against her own, and sucked in a small breath because the intimacy of their position wasn't lost on her. However, she was more concerned about the changes in his physique to worry about anything else right then.

She ran an exploratory hand down his back and frowned when she felt the ridges that marked each separate vertebra and rib. It was obvious that he'd had lost a great deal of weight in the past couple of years and she had no idea why. Had he been ill perhaps? She was just about to ask him when he suddenly stepped back and she was forced to release him.

'I'm sorry…again!' His voice was husky despite his attempts at levity and Holly's heart was immediately touched all over again. Maybe she *had* spent the last two years toughening herself up but it just wasn't possible to remain indifferent to him.

'You don't have to apologise, Ben.'

'Thanks.'

He didn't try to pretend that everything was fine and she was grateful for that. They had always tried to be honest with one another when they'd lived together, had made it a rule that they wouldn't lie to save face or each other's feelings. Even when Ben had told her he was leaving he hadn't lied about his reasons, as so many men might have done. It was strange because she hadn't realised before how much his honesty had meant to her.

'Is it something you want to talk about?' she asked, amazed that she could find anything positive about their parting when it had hurt so badly.

'Not really.'

'OK. But you are all right?' she insisted, because she needed to be sure. Maybe she *shouldn't* care how he felt but it simply wasn't possible to remain completely detached.

'I'm fine. Really. It's been one heck of a day, hasn't it?'

'It has,' she agreed, even though she doubted it was the pressure of work that had upset him. Ben was used to working long hours and dealing with the most traumatic incidents, too, but she'd never seen him so emotional before…

Apart from when he'd told her he was leaving her, of course.

Holly frowned as the memory surfaced with a rush. She rarely thought about that day because it was too painful, yet now she found herself wondering why Ben had appeared so distraught at the time. He'd taken the day off work because he'd had an appointment so she hadn't seen him since breakfast. He had been waiting for her when she'd got home after work and she'd known immediately that something had been wrong when he'd led her into the sitting room and asked her to sit down.

He had told her simply that he'd met someone else and that he was leaving her. He hadn't given her any details about the other woman, just said that he was sorry and that he'd never meant to hurt her. He'd been extremely tense and obviously worried when she hadn't said anything but at the time Holly had been too shocked to speak. She had never expected that Ben would leave her and had just sat there while her world had collapsed.

'So I'm really sorry, Holly, because I didn't bring you in here to start an argument.'

She jumped when she realised he'd been speaking. She quickly backtracked over what had happened and blushed when it struck her how childishly she'd behaved. The problem was that Ben had always managed to arouse her, and not only her temper either.

'And I'm sorry for the way I behaved just now,' she said swiftly, closing her mind to the thought because she couldn't deal with the memory of how wonderful their love-making had been. 'It was silly of me to get so het up.'

'So that makes it one apology apiece, discounting all my minor ones, of course. Do you want to go first and make it two, or shall I do the honours?'

Ben cocked his head on one side and regarded her quizzically. A tiny smile tugged at the corners of her mouth when she saw the laughter in his eyes.

'Oh, you can go first. After all, you probably have a lot more to apologise for than I do.'

'Oh, nice one! That slid very smoothly between the ribs.'

He grinned and Holly felt her pulse perform a determined little hiccup as she received the full benefit of the smile. It was hard to hide her dismay because she was no longer interested in Ben *that* way. She'd filed him under H for history just a few short hours ago and she wasn't about to have second thoughts because her hormones were playing up. So maybe he *was* the most handsome man she had ever met, and she *was* prepared to admit that, but she *wasn't* prepared to put her heart through the mincer a second time!

'I owe you an apology for the way I spoke about

Josh this morning. I had no right to comment on your relationship.'

'Josh and I don't have a relationship,' she replied without thinking. The fact that she wasn't one-hundred per cent certain that Ben couldn't hurt her again had to be faced. It would be both foolish and dangerous to dismiss the idea, as she'd done before.

'You don't? But why not? Sorry! It's none of my business, is it?' Ben sighed. 'That makes it three apologies to me and one to you.'

'It doesn't matter,' Holly assured him, because she certainly didn't want to make an issue out of it. Maybe it was silly but she felt uncomfortable about discussing her love life—or lack of one—with Ben. 'Josh and I are good friends but that's all. He's a really nice person and we get on extremely well but we aren't romantically involved.'

'Not yet.' Ben smiled but she could see a muscle in his jaw beating away, as though it was an effort for him to appear so upbeat at the prospect of her and Josh becoming an item in the future.

'No, not yet.' Her smile was a little too bright but she didn't want to think about why Ben should dislike the idea. As he'd said, it wasn't his business…

But? a small voice interjected. Because there'd been a definite *but* wriggling about on the end of that sentence.

Holly quickly dismissed the thought. There were no 'buts' in this situation. Getting hung up on the idea that Ben might care about her would be a mistake and she didn't intend to fall into that trap again.

'Sounds as though you have plans,' Ben observed with a laugh.

'Could be. Anyway, now that we've got the prickly bits over and done with, what did you want to say to me?' She quickly returned the conversation to the relatively safe topic of why he had seen fit to hijack her in the first place. She frowned when he didn't answer. 'Come on, Ben. Out with it.'

'I wanted to sort out a few things but I don't really think it's necessary now.'

'A few things? Like what? Whether or not I've got over you? Is that what you mean?'

'Mmm.' He grimaced. 'How big-headed can you get? I mean, why on earth would you still be pining for me, Holly? I bet you've had dozens of boyfriends in the last couple of years.'

'I've been out with a few people,' she replied coolly, because she had no intention of admitting that the 'few' added up to just two and that neither of them had been a *proper* relationship. Ben had been the first and the only man she'd ever slept with, although a team of mounties on horseback wouldn't have dragged that confession from her.

'Of course you have,' he agreed, obviously unperturbed by the idea of legions of men lining up to take her out.

It just went to prove how wrong she'd been to imagine he cared about her seeing Josh, Holly thought darkly. If Ben could handle the thought of her dating dozens of different men then one more wouldn't make a scrap of difference to him! The thought stung so much that it was an effort to appear calm when he continued.

'It's a weight off my mind, anyway.'

'Pardon?'

'The fact that you've moved on. I've been racking my brain to think of a way to…well, smooth things over between us, but obviously there's no need to worry. What happened in the past is all over and done with, isn't it, Holly?'

'Not quite.' His arrogance had almost left her speechless with shock. *Almost,* but not quite. She stood up straighter, not even trying to hide her contempt. Maybe he hadn't enjoyed upsetting her two years ago but he'd still gone ahead and dumped her, reneged on all those promises he'd made, broken her heart, and nothing he said or did now could change all of that.

'Yes, I'm over you, Ben, and, no, I am not still pining for you. However, if you seriously think I've forgiven you for the way you treated me then think again.' She laughed, relishing the expression of dismay that crossed his handsome face.

'But you said this morning that you were grateful to me?' he pointed out, and she consciously hardened her heart when she heard the consternation in his voice. All Ben *really* cared about was himself and she must never forget that. He didn't like to think that anyone thought badly of him.

'I know what I said and I meant it, too. However, that doesn't make up for the fact that you hurt me, Ben. You hurt me more than anyone will ever hurt

me again because I shall never, *ever* let myself love
anyone else as much as I loved you.'

'I don't know what to say…'

'There's nothing to say. That's just the way it is.
I can live with the situation so that's the end of the
matter as far as I'm concerned.'

She pushed past him but he caught hold of her
arm and swung her round to face him. His eyes were
filled with such pain that she almost weakened but
she couldn't afford to worry about his feelings.

'I'm sorry, Holly. I mean that from the bottom of
my heart. I'm truly sorry for what I did.'

'Apology accepted. That makes five, by my reck-
oning. I don't think I can match that, Ben, so I de-
clare you the winner.'

His face closed up when he heard the mockery in
her voice. He didn't say anything else as he let her
go. Holly left Resus and went to the staffroom for
her bag. Nicky and Josh were there, along with a
couple of the A and E staff. They were all going for
a drink to celebrate their first day and Holly immediately agreed to go with them. It would be better to
sit in a noisy pub than be on her own in the flat with
only her thoughts for company.

When Josh put his arm around her shoulders she
didn't protest and even managed a grin when Nicky
winked at her. There was nothing to stop her seeing
Josh—nothing and no one. Ben was just leaving
Resus and he stopped to let them pass, making some
excuse when Nicky invited him to join them.

Holly felt his eyes burning into her back as she
and Josh followed the others but she didn't look back

because looking back wasn't on her agenda. It was the future that mattered, what she did with the rest of her life. Falling in love with Ben might have been a painful episode but she'd learned a valuable lesson from it. No man would ever have the power to hurt her like that again.

CHAPTER FOUR

BY EIGHT o'clock that night Ben felt as though he would go mad if he didn't get out of his flat. The incessant thud of rock music thundering through the ceiling from the room above was making his head ache. He grabbed a sweater then ran downstairs and let himself out, breathing a sigh of relief when he was greeted by silence. He would have to find some place else to live if he intended to stay in Dalverston.

He sighed as he made his way along the road. He'd only just started the job and here he was thinking about leaving. Oh, he didn't *want* to leave because the job promised to be everything he'd hoped it would be. However, the cost of working in Dalverston might be too high. For him and for Holly. Holly had made it clear that she would never forgive him for the way he'd treated her and the thought of causing her any more distress was more than he could bear.

He reached the end of the road and stopped while he tried to decide which way to go. He'd had no chance to explore yet so wasn't familiar with the area. To his left all he could see was a road full of houses but when he looked to his right he spotted the river. The thought of a quiet stroll along the riverbank was definitely more appealing so he headed that way.

The sun was just dipping below the horizon when he reached the river. There were still a few people walking their dogs and he stopped to watch a handsome golden retriever jump into the water and fetch a stick its owner had thrown for it. He'd always fancied owning a dog like that, Ben thought as he watched the animal swimming back to the bank. It had been part of his dream for the future, along with a clutch of happy children and a cottage in the country. He and Holly had often talked about the family they would have and had decided that three would be the perfect number and that it wouldn't matter if they were girls or boys. It was unlikely that he would ever have a family now.

The thought caught him unawares and Ben had to breathe deeply as the enormity of it hit him. There'd be no children now, no dog or cottage in the country. There wouldn't be Holly either, and that was the worst thought of all. He'd sworn that he wouldn't allow himself to grow bitter about what had happened to him but it was hard, very hard indeed, to think about all that he'd lost through no fault of his own.

'Ben, are you OK?'

Holly's voice came floating towards him and Ben blinked. It was like a rerun of what had happened in Resus that afternoon so that for a moment he couldn't make sense of what was going on. And then he saw Holly walking purposefully towards him and stifled a groan as everything slotted back into its rightful sequence. Please, don't let this be round two in the beat-Ben-with-a-big-stick-for-his-past-transgressions routine, he thought desperately. He really didn't think he could handle another session like the last one.

'I'm fine,' he declared robustly, hoping that he might be able to deflect her. He pulled a wry face. 'Ever had the feeling that we've been here before?'

'Been here before?' she repeated, then suddenly laughed. 'Oh, I see! Well, don't worry because I promise not to make a habit of asking if you're all right. You are, though, aren't you?'

'I'm fine,' he reiterated, realising in surprise that it was true. Had it been that laugh which had worked its magic? The laugh allied to the thought that Holly might have softened just a little towards him since their last frosty encounter? He had no proof of that, of course, but it was better than having no hope at all of them ever finding peace.

'So what are you doing here? I thought you'd gone for a drink with the others,' he asked carefully, knowing he could be stepping onto dangerous ground. Even though he longed to know why Holly wasn't spending the evening with Josh, he didn't intend to risk disturbing their new-found harmony by asking her directly.

'I did but the pub was packed.' She shrugged. 'I had one drink then decided I needed some peace and quiet so left everyone to it and came down here instead.'

She started walking and, after a moment, Ben followed her. She didn't seem to dislike the idea of him accompanying her and that tiny seed of hope sprouted its first tender shoot. He racked his brain for something else to say that wouldn't cause offence but it was difficult to think of anything apart from the weather.

'It's a lovely evening—'

'It's really warm tonight—'

They both spoke at once and both stopped. Ben hid his smile because it was obvious that Holly was having as much trouble as he was in finding common ground. 'Ladies first,' he said with a heavy-handed gallantry which earned him a speaking look.

'I was just going to say how warm it is tonight.'

'It is. It's a really beautiful evening,' he replied, completely deadpan. They carried on walking and he could almost hear the cogs whirring as both he and Holly tried to come up with some more innocuous comments. Was she as worried about causing an argument as he was? he wondered, and felt his heart fill with tenderness at the thought.

'Do you live near here?' she asked at last.

'About five minutes away. Priory Lane—d'you know it?' he responded politely.

'I'm not sure… Is it where they're building those new flats?'

'I've no idea. I only arrived on Sunday night so I haven't had much of a chance to explore. I know where the local shops are so I can buy a loaf of bread and a newspaper but that's about it. I'm renting a bedsit in one of those old terraced houses, if that's any help.'

'A bedsit?' She stopped and stared at him and he could see the surprise in her eyes. 'Don't you find it rather cramped?'

'Cosy is how the estate agent described it when he showed me round,' he told her, his eyes twinkling with laughter. 'As he pointed out, there's less to clean with me having just the one room.'

'It sounds almost as bad as that flat we went to see when we were looking for a place in London. Do you remember that awful woman telling us that it was classed as a *bijou* residence?' She laughed and Ben felt his insides curl into knots of delight when he heard the amusement in her voice. It was so wonderful to know that she could find something good about their past life together.

'She opened what *we* thought was a cupboard and there was the bathroom.' She rolled her eyes. 'It was so tiny that you had to stand sideways because your shoulders wouldn't fit!'

'I remember all right. I would never have believed you could fit a living-room, a kitchen *and* a bathroom into a room that was ten feet long by ten feet wide if I hadn't seen it with my very own eyes.'

'It was incredible! And it wasn't as though it was cheap either. The monthly rent was almost as much as our combined salaries.' She shook her head. 'I don't know why I stayed in London for so long when I compare the price of accommodation there to what I'm paying now. Nicky and I share this beautiful flat and it doesn't cost a fraction of what I used to pay.'

'I'm hoping to find a decent place just as soon as I have the time to look around. It was all rather a rush when Sean phoned to tell me that I had the job so I settled for the first place the estate agent offered me.' He grimaced. 'I shall be a lot more choosy next time, believe me.'

'Well, you shouldn't have too much difficulty finding the ideal bachelor pad,' she said coolly. 'There's some new flats been built to cater for the staff working at the new business park and I believe they're very swish—lots of chrome and glass, that kind of thing.'

'Hmm, I'm not sure if that's what I'm after. What I'd really like is something with a bit of character for a change.'

'Low beams and roses round the door?' she suggested dryly.

'Something like that,' Ben replied, then briskly changed the subject because he wasn't comfortable with the turn the conversation had taken. It was barely five minutes since he'd been thinking about the rose-covered cottage he and Holly had once dreamed of owning and he didn't want to be reminded of that again. 'So what did you think of our first day? On a scale of one to ten, how would you rate it?'

'Oh, I'll have to think about that.'

She turned to stare across the river and Ben felt his pulse leap when he saw her lips purse as she considered his question. How many times had he seen her do that? he wondered, his stomach knotting painfully because he knew it was foolish to keep looking back. There was no point thinking about the past and wishing that things had turned out differently. He had to play the hand he'd been dealt and make the best of it.

'It has to be a definite ten for how interesting the day was,' she said at last. 'And ten again for the fact that I learnt such a lot. Then there's the excitement factor—that rush of adrenaline you get when you have to drop everything to go and save a life. That's another ten.'

'Sounds like high marks all round,' he observed softly, hoping she couldn't tell how difficult he was finding it to maintain his composure around her.

'Not quite. There were down parts to the day, bits that I'd have to award a low score to.'

Ben sighed because he knew without needing to ask which bits she meant. 'I feel really bad about what happened today, Holly. All I can say is that I had no idea you were working here when I took this job.'

'I'm sure you didn't, but would it really have made any difference to your decision, Ben?'

'What do you mean?' He turned towards her, wishing he knew where the question was leading.

'Would you *really* have turned it down if you'd known in advance that I was working here? And if so, why?' She turned as well so that they were facing each other and he could see the intensity in her eyes even though he couldn't understand the reason for it.

'I'd have thought twice about accepting it,' he said slowly, watching her face to see how she would react.

'But would you have turned it down in the end?' she insisted.

'I don't know.' He sighed when he saw the scepticism on her face. 'It's the truth, Holly. I have no idea what I would have done if I'd known we were going to have to work together. How about you? Would you have still taken the job if you'd realised there was a chance of seeing me again?'

Ben held his breath. He knew it was silly to attach too much importance to her answer but he couldn't help it. What it all boiled down to was whether or not Holly disliked him so much that she would have preferred to miss a wonderful career opportunity rather than have to work with him again.

'I don't know either, Ben, and I suppose it's point-less talking about it. What's done is done and we have to live with the decisions we've made—past and present.'

It was less than he'd wanted but more than he'd feared. Ben knew that he had to be content and not press her for anything more. 'Sounds as though we're in the same boat.'

'Seems like it. Anyway, I'd better get back. Nicky will wonder what's happened to me if she gets home and finds me missing.'

'I'll walk you back,' he offered at once, but she shook her head.

'There's no need. I only live across the road and nothing is going to happen to me,' she said lightly. However, it was obvious that she didn't want him looking after her. 'I'll see you tomorrow at work, I expect.'

'Yep. Expect so.'

He summoned a smile as she hurried away but it hurt to know how Holly felt about him. She may have allowed him to accompany her along the riverbank but that was as far as she was prepared to go. She didn't need him in her life and the thought filled him with the kind of despair he'd experienced two years ago when his life had fallen apart. If he could be granted just one wish then he knew it would be to recapture the magic he and Holly had shared, but it wasn't possible to go back to those days because too much had changed. To put it in the simplest of terms: he was no longer the man he used to be.

Life could be so bloody unfair at times!

'This is Adrienne Marshall. She's been suffering from severe abdominal pains during the night. She's also vomited several times since she was admitted.'

'Thanks, Kwame.'

Holly smiled at the handsome young black charge nurse as she went into the cubicle. It was just gone six and she'd been on duty for the whole of five minutes when Kwame had asked her to see the patient. The night staff were about to go off duty and there was the usual bustle in the department as the day staff arrived for the change-over. Ben was in a neighbouring cubicle with a three year-old who'd swallowed a bottle of vitamin tablets and the sound of the child's screams added to the general level of chaos.

'Sorry about the row,' she apologised, smiling at the young woman on the bed. 'The little fellow next door is none too happy by the sound of it. I'm Holly Daniels and I'm a doctor. Is the pain very severe?'

'Yes, it's dreadful and I feel so sick.' The young woman ran a trembling hand over her damp forehead. 'I've no idea what's wrong with me because I was fine last night.'

'Do you think it could be something you ate?' Holly suggested.

'I don't think so. I had cheese on toast for supper last night and I doubt that's what has caused it.'

'How about lunch?' Holly persisted, checking her chart. Adrienne's temperature had been rather high on admission so she made a note to check it again after she'd examined her.

'A carton of soup and a roll from the coffee-shop next door to where I work. I always go there for lunch because it's so handy,' Adrienne explained, looking distinctly green at the mention of food.

'Doesn't sound as though there's anything there to have caused food poisoning but we won't rule it out just yet. Let me take a look at you and see what I can find.' Holly drew back the sheet and carefully felt the young woman's abdomen, pausing when Adrienne groaned. 'Is it very tender there?'

'Yes. And my tummy feels sort of swollen, too.'

'When was your last period? Can you remember?'

'Last week.'

'And you've had no bleeding since then?' Holly continued, mentally running through possibilities such as an ectopic pregnancy. Ectopic pregnancies—where a foetus developed in a Fallopian tube rather than inside the womb—could cause intense abdominal pain like the patient was suffering but was usually accompanied by heavy vaginal bleeding. Adrienne shook her head. 'No. And I had my appendix out when I was a child, too.'

'Which was going to be my next question, only you beat me to it!'

Holly smiled as she turned to Kwame and asked him to check Adrienne's temperature again. She glanced at her notes and frowned as she considered what she'd learned so far. 'So, no bleeding and no appendix to worry about either. Any signs of diarrhoea?'

'No, thank heavens!' Adrienne replied with a grimace.

'Mmm, I sympathise.' Holly laughed. 'You've enough to contend with at the moment without adding to your woes, haven't you?'

She paused while Kwame told her the patient's temperature then continued. 'Your temperature is certainly higher than it should be and that suggests you may have some kind of an infection. Have you experienced any problems urinating, maybe a burning pain or stinging sensation when you pass water?'

'No, nothing like that. I've had cystitis in the past, if that's what you mean, and this is completely different. I feel so sore...'

The young woman suddenly broke off and Holly grabbed a dish as she vomited. She handed Adrienne a tissue afterwards and smiled reassuringly. 'Just try to relax. I'd like to give you an internal examination to see what's going on. You'll feel more comfortable if you lie on your back with your legs bent.'

She made Adrienne comfortable then pulled on some gloves and examined her. It was immediately apparent that her vagina was too tender to carry out more than a cursory check so Holly kept it brief, taking a vaginal swab while she was at it.

'I'm going to arrange for some blood tests to be done, Adrienne,' she explained while Kwame covered the woman with a sheet. 'They'll help to pinpoint the source of the problem. I know you said that you had a period last week but I just want to be sure that you haven't suffered a miscarriage recently or maybe had a termination.'

'Of course not!' Adrienne denied, obviously horrified by the suggestion.

'I have to ask these questions if I'm to find out what's wrong with you,' Holly explained gently.

'I know and I'm sorry because I didn't mean to bite your head off like that. I just feel so awful.'

'I understand. Don't worry about it.' Holly patted her hand then drew Kwame aside and told him what she needed done. 'I want a blood test plus a culture from the vaginal swab. We'll put her on a saline drip and give her broad-spectrum antibiotics for now. Once we know for certain what's wrong with her, we can tailor the drugs to the infection.'

'What do you think might be wrong with her?' Kwame asked quietly.

'I'm wondering if it's salpingitis. The symptoms certainly point towards it. Severe abdominal pain and vaginal tenderness are classic signs of inflammation of the Fallopian tubes. We'll need to keep her here while we find out what's going on so can you check if there's a bed available in the assessment ward? She'll also need pain relief while we wait for the lab to get back to us.'

She wrote down the dosages of the drugs on the chart then went to speak to Adrienne again. 'We're going to move you to the assessment ward while we wait for the lab results. Kwame will give you something for the pain so I want you to try and rest. Once the lab gets back to us, we'll have a better idea what we're dealing with. In the meantime, is there anyone you'd like me to contact?'

'My boyfriend, Paul Wood. He was away on business last night.' Adrienne gave her the name and the phone number of the hotel where her boyfriend was staying. 'He'll be worried sick when he hears what's happened to me.'

'Don't worry, I'll be careful how I break the news to him,' Holly assured her as she jotted the details on her pad. She left the cubicle and went to the office to make the call. The hotel's switchboard put her straight through to the man's room but nobody answered. Holly checked her watch as she hung up. It was barely six-thirty but maybe he'd gone to breakfast early. She made a note to try again later then looked round when Mandy Johnson, the triage nurse, tapped on the door and asked her to see another patient.

That seemed to set the pattern for the morning because it was non-stop from then on although there were no calls for the rapid response team. Ben was also kept busy so she saw him only briefly in passing, not that she was sorry. She had regretted their walk along the riverbank as soon as she'd got home, and had made up her mind there wouldn't be a repeat performance. Although nothing had happened, it had left her feeling so on edge that she'd had problems sleeping.

Of course, her restlessness could have been attributed to excitement at the first day in a new job, but Holly was too honest to pretend that was the real reason. It had been seeing Ben again that had done the damage, working with him during the day then walking with him beside the river last night. At the time she hadn't given any thought to what she'd been doing but later she'd realised it had been a mistake to spend time with him away from work. She and Ben were no longer involved and she mustn't forget that.

Lunchtime arrived at last and Holly was starving as she made her way to the canteen. Mandy had commandeered a table for the A and E staff so she carried her tray over there and plonked herself down on a chair.

'I am bushed! I thought it was tiring yesterday, rushing about all over the place, but it's been just as bad this morning. What's going on? Are we giving away freebies to everyone who visits A and E?'

'Some of the people I've seen today should sign up for loyalty cards. They spend almost as much time there as I do,' Mandy remarked with a grin. 'I don't know where I'm going wrong. I've tried treating them mean but they keep coming back for more!'

'That's because they need a very firm hand,' Kwame put in, smiling at the pretty young nurse.

'Shame it doesn't work with colleagues,' Mandy retorted, blushing.

Holly smiled to herself as she peeled the wrapping

off a soggy egg and tomato sandwich. It looked like there might be a romance brewing there. She bit into the chewy white bread, thinking about the dynamics of the team. Sean was happily married and so were Max, Helen and Judith—the latter the two senior staff nurses. As for the rest of the team, they were either dating or in long-term relationships. That left just Nicky, Josh, Ben and herself as the odd ones out in the romance stakes. The very nature of their job meant that most people ended up dating someone they worked with, so would Ben and Nicky end up going out together perhaps?

Holly felt her stomach churn and put her sandwich back on the plate. It was silly to get upset at the thought of Ben dating her flatmate but she couldn't seem to help it. She glanced round when the canteen door opened and bit her lip when she saw Ben coming in. Was she *really* over him, or had she been deluding herself?

CHAPTER FIVE

BEN could feel the chill in the atmosphere as soon as he sat down. It just so happened that the only free seat was next to Holly and he could feel the frosty vibes flowing his way. He glanced at her and sighed when she deliberately looked the other way. He'd hoped the situation might have improved after last night but obviously not. He'd just have to play Mr Nice Guy a bit longer, he decided as he unravelled his sandwich from its plastic cocoon, and hope she'd realise eventually that she had nothing to fear from him.

'What's it like?' he asked, smiling winsomely when Holly reluctantly glanced at him.

'What's what like?' she countered in a voice that sounded as though she'd been sucking lemons all morning.

'The sandwich.' He grimaced as he picked up the two floppy pieces of bread. 'Although I hardly need to ask when it looks as though it died a painful death a couple of days ago.'

'The food here isn't too bad normally,' Mandy put in helpfully. 'It's not exactly cordon bleu but it's palatable—well, most of the time anyway.'

'Sounds like a definite improvement on some of the places I've worked.' Ben took a bite out of the sandwich. 'I don't know what they do to the food in some hospitals but everything tastes like boiled bandages. Remember that lasagne they used to serve at the Free, Holly? It was disgusting.'

He chewed the mouthful of bread then reached for his can of cola and suddenly realised that everyone was staring at him. 'What's wrong?' he asked, mystified by the expressions on all their faces, all except Holly's, that was, because he could read her expression without any difficulty.

Why on earth was she glowering at him like that? Ben wondered, hastily backtracking over the conversation, and bit back a groan of dismay when he realised what he'd said.

'I didn't know that you and Holly used to work together!' Mandy exclaimed, obviously voicing everyone's thoughts.

'Didn't you?'

Ben managed a sickly smile but he could have kicked himself for the slip. He had no idea what Holly's reasons had been for staying quiet about their past relationship but he knew why *he* hadn't wanted it to become public knowledge. Snippets of information had a nasty habit of joining up and he didn't want people finding out what had happened to him. He certainly didn't relish the thought of the people he worked with feeling *sorry* for him!

'I don't suppose it ever cropped up before,' he said with a determined attempt at nonchalance. 'It certainly isn't a secret. We worked together in London for quite some time, didn't we, Holly?'

'Two years. Ben was a registrar when I was a very young and very naïve houseman.'

'Not that naïve,' he countered, his smile firmly anchored into place. If she was trying to imply that he'd taken advantage of her then she wasn't getting away with it. Maybe he *had* made the running by asking her out but Holly had been just as keen as him to further their relationship.

The thought of exactly how keen they'd both been made his blood heat but he ignored the rapid rise in his temperature as he turned to her. He was willing to accept the blame for hurting her, but he wasn't willing to accept that he'd used his age and his position to seduce her.

'You had most of the male members of the department in a spin, as I recall. They were practically falling over themselves to ask you out on a date.'

'Doesn't sound as though much has changed,' Lara Walters, one of the junior nurses, put in with a grin. 'Our Holly still knocks 'em dead. The rest of us don't get a look in when she's around!'

Everyone laughed but Ben was relieved when the conversation moved on to a different topic. He glanced at Holly but she was munching away at her sandwich and ignoring him. It was difficult to tell what was going through her head but he knew that he wouldn't rest until he'd made sure that she wouldn't tell anyone about their affair. When she pushed back her chair, he got up as well.

'I'll come down with you, Holly. There's a couple of things I need to ask you about,' he announced, deeming it wiser not to try to hide the fact that he wanted to speak to her. The more open they were, the less people would speculate. Maybe it was selfish but he desperately wanted to avoid arousing any interest in his private life. Sean knew what had happened but no one else did and that was the way Ben intended it to continue. Discussing how close he'd come to dying wasn't exactly his favourite topic of conversation.

'I'm going to the loo so I'm afraid it will have to wait until later,' she replied, picking up her tray and heading across the canteen at a rate of knots.

Ben quickly loaded his own tray but by the time he'd stacked it in the rack by the door, Holly had disappeared. He hurried into the corridor and caught up with her. 'Look, this will only take a minute but first I want to say that I'm sorry about what just happened. I didn't mean to let that slip out.'

'Forget it.'

She carried on walking, leaving him with little choice other than to follow her. Ben's mouth thinned because he wasn't in the habit of trotting after a woman like a wretched *lapdog*. She pushed open the door to the ladies' lavatories and disappeared inside but he was damned if he was going to let her escape that easily.

Ben followed her inside, smiling an apology to a couple of nurses who were on their way out. 'Sorry about this, ladies. I just need a word with someone.'

He heard the women laugh as the door swung to and gritted his teeth. Bearing in mind that he'd been anxious to avoid any gossip, he wasn't exactly making a success of this. It would be all over the hospital by the end of the day that he'd followed Holly into the women's loos! The thought was like the proverbial red rag to the bull so he was in no mood to compromise when he rounded the corner and was confronted by a furious Holly.

'What on earth do you think you're doing, Ben? It's bad enough that you told everyone that we knew one another, but to come trailing in here after me…'

'If you'd tried being a bit more reasonable and listened to what I had to say then I wouldn't have needed to follow you. I only wanted a couple of minutes of your time but, oh, no, you couldn't even spare me that.'

'Why should I do what you want? You don't own me, Ben Carlisle. You can't give me orders *or* demand that I listen to you, and the sooner you get that into your head, the better it will be for both of us!'

'I don't believe I'm hearing this.' He slapped his forehead with the palm of his hand. 'Although heaven knows why I'm surprised. You were always the same. Once you got yourself all fired up, logic flew straight out of the window. You have to be the most unreasonable woman I've ever met!'

'Thank you very much. I shall take that as a compliment. Now, if you'll excuse me, I did come in here for a reason.'

'And I followed you for an even better one!'

Ben knew he was making a mess of things but it was hard to remain calm when Holly seemed determined to behave so irrationally. Surely she must know that he would *never* have followed her if it hadn't been important that he speak to her?

Buoyed up by a feeling of self-righteousness, he fixed her with a steely-eyed glare which wavered when he saw what looked suspiciously like tears in her eyes. It was an effort to remember what he'd wanted to say because the thought that he'd upset her had thrown him off track.

'I would prefer it if people didn't find out about our relationship, Holly. I have my reasons, of course, but suffice to say that I don't think it would be in either of our interests to have everyone gossiping about us.'

'They won't hear about it from me, I assure you.'

Her voice sounded decidedly husky and Ben frowned because he didn't know whether to apologise for upsetting her or pretend he hadn't noticed. He sighed because dealing with Holly seemed to be fraught with problems and he couldn't help comparing what was happening now to how it had been in the past. Then they had spent hours talking to each other. They hadn't always agreed, of course, but even their arguments had been fun, especially when they'd made up afterwards…

He quickly erased that thought before it could cause even more problems. 'Thanks. I appreciate that.'

'Don't mention it. Is that it, then? There's nothing else you want to say to me?'

'No.' He shrugged. 'I just thought it best to make my position clear.'

'And you have. Don't worry, Ben, I understand perfectly.'

The catch in her voice was almost his undoing. Ben didn't say anything else as he quickly left. Knowing that Holly was upset and that it was his fault was more than he could bear and he was terrified that he would do something stupid. There was just no point wishing he could take her in his arms and promise her that he would take care of her because he wasn't in a position to make promises like that. It was the reason why he had let her go two years ago and it still applied even now. It hadn't been a lack of love that had made him end their affair— just the opposite. He had loved her too much to ruin her life and the worst thing of all was knowing that he could never tell her that.

Holly went straight to the assessment ward as soon as she got back to A and E. Adrienne Marshall's lab results had arrived while she'd been at lunch and she wanted to speak to Adrienne herself rather than leave it to someone else. It also meant that she could avoid seeing Ben for a while which was a definite bonus.

Holly sighed as she pushed open the door to the ward. It was silly to get so upset but she couldn't help it. Ben had seemed so anxious to prevent anyone finding out about their relationship that she couldn't help wondering if he was ashamed of what had happened. The thought that he might be embarrassed because they'd had an affair hurt. She had loved him with all her heart and yet he thought of her now as nothing more than a mistake.

'Do you know what's wrong with me yet, Dr Daniels?'

Holly put aside her own problems as she stopped beside Adrienne's bed. Adrienne was looking much better now thanks to the antibiotics and analgesics she'd received. However, Holly knew the test results would probably upset her and chose her words with care.

'It seems that it's what I suspected, Adrienne. Your white-cell count is very high which indicates that you have an infection and that's caused salpingitis—inflammation of one of your Fallopian tubes.'

'Oh, dear! How on earth has that happened?' Adrienne exclaimed in dismay.

'There are a number of causes,' Holly said carefully. 'Salpingitis can be caused by an infection caught during childbirth, miscarriage or termination. However, we ruled out all of those before, didn't we? The most common cause is a sexually transmitted disease such as a chlamydial infection or gonorrhoea.'

'But that's ridiculous! I can't have caught something like that. I've only ever slept with my boyfriend, Paul. You must have got it wrong!'

'The lab is doing a culture from the vaginal swab I took from you earlier and that will confirm it, one way or the other,' Holly said quietly. 'I know how difficult this must be for you, Adrienne. However, if it does turn out that the infection is the result of a sexually transmitted disease then you must have caught it from someone.'

'Then I must have caught it off Paul. So that means he's been sleeping with someone else, doesn't it?' the girl said slowly. Her eyes suddenly welled with tears. 'He said that he loved me and I believed him, too!'

'Some STDs can remain undetected for quite a

while so it's important not to jump to any hasty con-
clusions. However, if the lab results do prove that
it's gonorrhoea or a chlamydial infection then your
boyfriend will need treatment as well. And so will
any other person he may have been in contact with
recently,' she added diplomatically.

'What did Paul say when you told him I was in
hospital?' Adrienne asked brokenly.

'I didn't actually speak to him. I phoned the hotel
but he wasn't in his room,' Holly explained gently.
'Would you like me to try again?'

'Please.' Adrienne rubbed her hands over her face.
'I did wonder when he said that he had to go away
on business again this week. It's the third time it's
happened in the past month. D'you think he's been
seeing someone else and he's just used that as an
excuse?'

'I really don't know. That's something you will
need to ask him, I'm afraid.'

Holly sighed as she left the ward. It sounded as
though Adrienne might be right in her suspicions but
who was she to say for certain? She'd had no idea
that Ben had been seeing someone else because he'd
never spent any nights away from her—apart from
when he'd been working, of course.

She frowned as she went to make the phone call
because that thought, naturally, had led to another.
When had Ben found the time to see someone else?
He'd worked the same ridiculously long hours that
she'd worked so free time had been at a premium.
When he'd been out at night, working, that's exactly
what he had been doing, as the rosters would prove.

She could account for almost every single minute of the time they'd been together so when had he had the chance to carry on an affair?

It was a question she'd never asked herself before yet all of a sudden Holly knew that it needed answering.

The afternoon was every bit as busy as the morning had been so she didn't have a chance to speak to Ben about it. There were two calls for the rapid response team in quick succession. Josh and Nicky had only just left, in fact, when the second call came through. Sean was in a meeting that afternoon so Holly hurried to the office when she heard the phone ringing but Ben was already there.

'What have we got?' she asked as she went in.

'Serious RTA just outside town,' he explained, tapping notes into the computer. Each call they received had to be logged into the system the minute it arrived. It was vital that a record was kept of which members of staff were responding and what vehicles they were using so that Ambulance Control always knew what services were available. Holly waited patiently while he finished inputting the necessary information, smiling wryly as she watched him hunting around the keyboard for every letter. Ben might have many skills to his credit but typing wasn't one of them.

'That's *that* done,' he announced in obvious relief, looking up. He must have seen the amusement on her face because he frowned. 'What's the matter?'

'Nothing. I was just admiring your expertise on

the keyboard. You have a very distinctive style, if I may say so.'

'It's called the one-fingered hunt and peck method.' He flexed his right index finger. 'Sheer poetry in motion, isn't it?'

He grinned at her and Holly felt her spirits suddenly lift. It felt good to be able to laugh with Ben about something so ridiculous after the frosty exchange they'd had earlier. She realised with a jolt how much she'd missed his quirky sense of humour so that it was an effort to concentrate as he led the way from the office. She didn't want to remember all his good points when it would only serve to confuse her even more.

'Do we have any details about who's been injured?' she asked, purposely confining her thoughts to the current situation.

'An eight-year-old boy.' He grabbed a safety helmet off the shelf and tossed it to her. 'Apparently, there was a demonstration being held today about some new landfill site that's been opened on the outskirts of the town. The people who are opposed to the site had put up barriers to stop the lorries going in and out. One guy tried to drive around them and somehow managed to knock down a child in the process.'

'Why have they asked us to respond?' Holly queried, slipping on a protective suit over her clothes. She popped and zipped then glanced at him. 'Surely the regular paramedics could have dealt with this?'

'The kid is trapped under the lorry and it could be a while before they get him out so they decided it would be best if there was a doctor present.' He zipped the front of his own suit. 'Plus there's a massive traffic jam building up because of all the lorries that were using the landfill site. It will take a while for an ambulance to get there but we'll be able to take the back route over Dalverston moor.'

'Oh, I see.'

Holly didn't ask anything else as she quickly led the way to the garage. Time was of the essence in dealing with this type of situation and she was just glad they were able to respond now she knew how serious it was. The four-wheel-drive was all ready and waiting for them so she slid into the passenger seat while Ben took the wheel. The landfill site was just a ten-minute drive from the hospital normally but they had to take a circuitous route to avoid the traffic. They still made good time, however, so it wasn't long before they arrived.

Ben parked the vehicle then forged a way through the crowd and headed straight for the lorry. The driver was sitting on the grass verge with a policeman standing beside him. He seemed dazed when Holly knelt down beside him. Ben had gone to speak to the officer in charge so she concentrated on the driver's injuries.

'I'm a doctor from Dalverston General Hospital,' she explained. She tipped back the man's head and studied the gash on his left temple. 'You've had a bit of bump from the look of things. Did you black out at all?'

'No. I'm fine. It's the little lad you need to worry

about.' The man took a gulping breath. 'I didn't see him. I just didn't see him!'

'Just try to stay calm,' Holly told him, taking a dressing out of her bag and taping it over the wound. She found a torch and checked his eyes but there were no obvious signs of head trauma so she left him with the policeman. Another police officer called her over to his car and asked her to take a look at the boy's mother. Holly quickly introduced herself but the woman was too upset to respond. She clutched Holly's hand, her eyes brimming with tears.

'I should never have brought Ryan here! It's all my fault, isn't it? If I hadn't brought him then he wouldn't have got hurt…'

She couldn't go on and Holly gently squeezed her hand. 'We're going to do everything we can to help your son. I promise you that. Now, did the lorry hit you as well?'

The woman shook her head. 'No, I'm all right. It's Ryan who needs you, Doctor.'

'Then I'll go and see what I can do to help.' Holly left her in the police car and went to find Ben. He'd finished speaking to the officer in charge and her heart sank when she saw how grim he looked.

'How's the child?' she asked, glancing towards the lorry. Its front wheels were suspended over a deep drainage ditch which ran alongside the road and she could see that the fire crew were placing blocks against its rear wheels to stop it rolling forwards.

'I can't tell. He's trapped under the front axle from what I can gather. They're going to use air bags to raise the cab so they can get him out but I've no idea how long that's going to take. I need to get underneath the lorry to check how badly injured he is.'

'That sounds very risky!' she exclaimed. She glanced at the lorry again and shivered as she imagined what would happen if it slid further into the ditch. Anyone underneath it at the time would be crushed.

'It's the only way. I certainly can't hang around here until they pull him out.'

Ben didn't waste any more time debating the point as he strode back to the lorry. Holly saw him confer with one of the firemen and could tell the man was warning him how dangerous it would be to crawl beneath the lorry while it was so precariously balanced. The warning had little effect, however, so her heart was in her mouth as she watched Ben drop into the ditch and wriggle his way beneath the massive vehicle.

She ran over and knelt down beside the cab, wanting to be ready in case he needed her help. The child was lying partly in the ditch so that all she could see was the back of his head. There was barely enough room for Ben to move but she saw him reach out and touch the child, obviously checking for a pulse. He looked round and spotted her peering under the side of the cab.

'Pulse is thready. His left femur is broken and he's lost a lot of blood so he's probably in shock.'

'Can we get a drip into him?' she suggested, although she'd already guessed what the answer would be.

'No chance. I'd never be able to get a line into

him. There's not enough room to manoeuvre under here—'

He broke off when the lorry suddenly shuddered. Holly gasped in dismay when she realised that part of the ditch wall had given way under its weight. 'Are you all right?' she called, frantically peering into the appreciably smaller gap beneath the cab. *'Ben?'*

'I'm OK,' he called back, his voice slightly muffled. 'I'll feel a lot better once I'm out of here, though.'

'You and me both,' she muttered in relief, quickly moving out of the way so the firemen could get on with fitting the airbags beneath the cab. The next ten minutes were extremely tense. Ben insisted on staying with the child and all she could do was to stand and watch while the lorry was raised one excruciatingly slow inch at a time. Her nerves were positively screaming by the time the boy was freed and Ben scrambled out of the ditch. She hurriedly turned away because she couldn't take the risk of him seeing how scared she'd been. If Ben realised how worried she'd been about him then he'd be bound to wonder why and she wasn't sure she could explain it to him.

Fortunately, there was no time to dwell on how she felt as they prepared the child for the journey to hospital. He'd suffered a compound fracture of his left femur so Ben covered the area with a dressing to minimise the risk of infection then placed the limb in a splint while she set up a drip.

'We'll just do the basics here,' he instructed, fastening the Velcro straps on the splint. 'There's no point wasting time. The sooner we get him to Resus the better.'

'Fine, whatever you say,' she agreed, happy for once to let him take charge. There was no way that she was going to argue with him about issuing orders when it was in the child's best interests. Anyway, he'd earned the right to call the shots after putting his own life at risk like that, she thought, trying to quell the shudder that ran through her at the thought of the danger he'd been in.

An ambulance arrived just as they finished strapping Ryan to a spinal board so they helped the paramedics load him into the back. The police were providing an escort through the traffic and they set off with sirens wailing and lights flashing. Ben hastily gathered up their equipment and stuffed it back into the bag then ran to their vehicle. Holly was hard on his heels but even so she only just had time to scramble inside before he started the engine.

'D'you think he'll make it?' she asked, shooting him a sidelong glance as he turned the car round in a tight circle.

'I hope so,' he replied grimly.

He didn't say anything else as they drove back to the hospital but she could see the determination on his face and knew that he would do everything in his power to save the child. The ambulance arrived just a few minutes after them so they rushed Ryan straight through to Resus where Ben started rattling out orders.

'I want his sats done a.s.a.p. He's lost a lot of

blood so we'll need samples for cross-matching, stat! And page Alison and tell her that we'll need X-rays. Right, everyone, on my count—one, two, three.'

They quickly shifted the boy onto a bed and Holly began to examine him. Ben was taking off his filthy overalls before scrubbing his hands and she knew he'd want an initial report as soon as he'd finished. The boy was still unconscious but his eyes responded when she shone a light into them so she ruled out any major head trauma for the moment.

'Head OK?' Ben asked, snapping on a fresh pair of gloves as he came to the bed.

'Seems to be,' Holly replied just as briefly, sliding her hand under the child's back so she could check his spine. This initial assessment was vital if they were to give the boy the best chance possible of re-covering. She knew how easy it was to miss a life-threatening injury in the heat of the moment and was determined that wasn't going to happen after Ben's recent heroic efforts. She carefully felt her way along the vertebrae and shook her head. 'Spine feels OK but we'll need an X-ray to be on the safe side.'

'So far, so good,' Ben muttered, waiting impa-tiently while Lara finished cutting away the last of the boy's clothing.

Holly didn't answer as she moved on to the child's collarbone, determined that nothing was going to es-cape her. She grimaced when her fingers immediately detected an irregularity. 'Fractured left clavicle,' she said, glancing at Ben who was now examining the child's lower body.

'And possible fracture of the pelvis as well. It definitely doesn't feel right. If the pelvis is fractured then there could be damage to the bladder, which means he'll need immediate surgery.' He turned to Lara. 'Page Max and warn him that we'll be sending the kid through as soon as we've finished stabilising him. I don't want there to be any hold-ups if we can avoid them.'

'Do you think there could be other internal injuries as well as the bladder?' Holly asked, gently feeling her way down the child's arms.

'I'd say it's extremely likely.' Ben pursed his lips as he studied the monitor screen. 'His pressure's way down and although it could be the blood he's lost from that femur, I'd put my money on internal bleeding. Let's increase the drip and get some more fluid into him. That should bring his pressure up with a bit of luck.'

He glanced round when the door opened and Alison Hart, their radiographer, appeared. 'Can you do the usual X-rays, please—lateral cervical spine and anteroposterior views of the chest and pelvis? It seems likely there are pelvic fractures so we'll leave the rest till later because we need to get him to Theatre.'

'Will do,' Alison replied with her usual cheerfulness. She quickly positioned the ceiling-mounted radiographic equipment until it was directly above the special trauma bed which had been designed to allow for X-rays to be taken *in situ* and took the pictures as soon as the staff were safely out of the way. 'Give me a couple of minutes and I'll have them on the screen for you,' she told them, hurrying to the computer terminal.

Holly went back to the bed and checked the child's responses again, using the Glasgow coma scale which involved awarding points for eye opening and both motor and verbal responses. She glanced at Ben. 'His score doesn't seem to have dropped.'

'That's something to be grateful for,' he replied shortly, busily examining the child's left thigh where the bone was protruding through the flesh. A large flap of skin had been ripped away and he shook his head. 'What a mess! He's going to need the plastics people to sort this out.'

'Max will arrange that,' Holly assured him. Alison came over to tell them the X-rays were ready so she went to look at them. 'You were right about the pelvis,' she called over her shoulder. 'The pubis bone is fractured on both sides and it looks like the bladder is damaged from this area of clouding.'

'Let's have a look.' Ben came and stood behind her so he could study the screen and Holly had to fight the sudden urge to move out of the way when she felt the heat from his body all down her spine. 'Mmm, it's just as I suspected. Traffic accidents are the most common cause of damage to the bladder in both children and adults.'

He leant closer to the monitor and she froze when she felt his chest touching her shoulder blades. All of a sudden she was reminded of that question she'd asked herself at lunchtime: *How could she be over him when she responded to his nearness this way?*

It was impossible to answer it so it was a relief

when Lara came to tell them that Theatre was ready and Ben moved away. They went back to the bed and Holly made a determined effort to concentrate while she checked the child's vital signs once more. 'BP marginally better than it was and his sats have improved, too. Pulse is also steadier.'

'Then let's get him out of here.' Ben nodded to Kwame, who immediately came over and took charge. He sighed as he watched the child being wheeled out of the door on his way to Theatre. 'All we can do now is pray that he makes it. Maybe it was an accident but it doesn't seem right that a young life should have been put needlessly in jeopardy.'

Holly frowned when she saw the regret on his face. Ben had been totally focused and wholly professional while he'd been working but there was no denying that he looked genuinely upset. Was it just because this case had involved a child and dealing with injured children was always more emotive? Or was there another reason why he should be so moved by the boy's plight?

Frankly, she had no idea what the answer was. It was just another mystery to add to all the others and suddenly she knew that she couldn't wait any longer to find out what was going on. She drew Ben aside so the rest of the staff couldn't overhear what she had to say.

'Look, Ben, there's a couple of things I need to ask you. Is there any chance we could meet up tonight after work?'

'What kind of things are we talking about?' he said slowly.

'Just things.' She shrugged but she could sense his reluctance. 'You said that you wanted to resolve this situation but I don't think we can until we clear up a few points that have been puzzling me recently.'

'I see. So, what did you have in mind?' he asked with a marked lack of enthusiasm.

Holly frowned because she couldn't understand why he was so hesitant. He'd been keen enough to clear the air before and she'd been the one who'd hung back, but all of a sudden their positions seemed to have reversed. Why? Because there was something he wanted to hide?

Her heart lurched at the thought of what she might uncover but, no matter how painful it turned out to be, she had to know the truth. She looked round and nodded when Kwame poked his head round the door to warn them that another patient was on the way then turned back to Ben again. 'Just a drink and a chat, that's all—nothing heavy. There's a pub just along the road from here so we could go there.'

He shook his head. 'I'd prefer it if we could meet somewhere nobody will see us.'

'Oh, right.' It was hard to hide her dismay. Did he have to make it so obvious that he was ashamed of being seen with her? 'In that case, would you like to come round to the flat? Nicky is on a late today and won't be back until eleven so that should give you plenty of time to make your escape without being seen.'

Ben sighed when he heard the edge in her voice. 'I just don't think it's a good idea to start people gossiping. It's in your best interests as well as mine, Holly.'

'Right, fine. Whatever,' she agreed as though it didn't matter a jot, although it did. 'So is that a yes, then?'

'Yes. All right. What time d'you want me to be there?'

'Shall we make it eight o'clock?'

She gave him her address then went out to wait for the ambulance. Normally she loved her job but all of a sudden she was impatient for the day to end. She couldn't explain it but she had a feeling that Ben's answers to all those questions that had been troubling her of late would affect the rest of her life, which was crazy really. Up until a few days ago she'd had her life all mapped out but now it felt as though everything was up in the air. Seeing Ben again had upset the status quo but she had to keep a clear head and not do anything stupid. She just needed to know the truth and then she would be able to draw a line under the past.

It all sounded so simple in theory but, as she watched the ambulance turning into the drive, Holly knew that nothing about her relationship with Ben could be classed as simple. Her feelings for him were very, very complicated indeed.

CHAPTER SIX

BEN called at the corner shop for a bottle of wine on his way to Holly's that night. There wasn't much of a selection so it was a choice of either chilled Chardonnay or warm Chablis. In the end he opted for the Chablis because Holly had always loathed Chardonnay. Maybe he should get some nibbles to go with it, he thought, looking around the shelves. Olives or some of those salted nuts Holly loved. He was just about to ask the shopkeeper if he had any in stock when it struck him what he was doing.

Ben paid for the wine and hurriedly left. This wasn't a *social* occasion and he wasn't going to Holly's to spend the evening reminiscing about old times. She wanted some questions answered and he was going to have to be very careful what he said. He couldn't afford any more slip-ups like the one he'd made that lunchtime. If she found out *why* he'd lied about his reasons for ending their relationship then there was no knowing what she might do. He couldn't take the chance of her feeling so sorry for him that she would offer to try again.

The thought of becoming the object of her pity was very hard to swallow. Ben walked the rest of the way, wishing that he'd never agreed to see her that night. He rang the bell and felt panic hit him when he heard her voice coming over the intercom.

How could he be sure that he wouldn't weaken and
tell her the truth? Maybe he didn't want to become
an object of pity but was he sure that he'd be able
to resist if there was a chance they could try again?

'Yes?'

The impatience in her voice sliced through his
thoughts. 'It's me, Holly,' he informed her, struggling to get a grip on himself as she buzzed him in.
Getting back with Holly wasn't an option and didn't
even rate a mention on his extremely short list of
things to be done in the future. What he had to do
now was tidy up a few loose ends and that would be
it.

Ben's resolve stiffened as he made his way to her
flat. She'd left the front door open so he went straight
in. A tiny entrance hall led into a surprisingly large
sitting-room and he sighed with envy as he looked
around. 'This *is* nice. It looks so huge after my poky
little bedsit.'

'It is a lovely room,' she agreed politely. 'We face
south so it's always lovely and bright in here.'

'So I can see. Did you have to decorate or was it
like this when you moved in?' he asked, admiring
the cream-coloured walls and pale wooden flooring,
such a contrast to the hideous orange paintwork and
purple shag-pile that adorned his current abode.

'We repainted the walls but that was basically it.
We've not had the time to do very much else to the
place,' she explained, tossing back her hair as she
looked around the room.

Ben felt his pulse immediately quicken as his attention suddenly shifted away from his surroundings

and centred on Holly instead. She had changed out of her work clothes into olive-green cargo trousers and a buff-coloured top which left several inches of her slim midriff bare. She'd unpinned her hair as well and the glossy chestnut curls swirled around her shoulders in a glorious tangle.

Despite his resolve to remain impartial, Ben couldn't help thinking how lovely she looked with the creamy walls providing the perfect backdrop for her vibrant beauty. His gaze skimmed appreciatively over her slender body only stopping when he came to her bare feet, and he chuckled when he saw that her toenails were painted the most amazing shade of green.

'I see you still have a fetish for painting your toenails crazy colours.'

'I…um…yes.'

She sounded disconcerted by the comment and Ben cursed himself for passing such a personal remark. He had to remember that comments like that were off limits if he was to get through the evening unscathed. He quickly handed over the carrier bag, deeming it safer to stick to the accepted pleasantries between guest and host.

'I bought this for us to drink. Sorry it's warm but there wasn't much of a choice, I'm afraid. It was either chilled Chardonnay or warm Chablis and I know how you loathe Chardonnay.'

'I don't mind it, actually,' she replied stiffly.

'My mistake,' he apologised, although he was beginning to realise just how difficult this was going to be when it was obvious that any references to their shared past of a *personal* nature were strictly taboo. He found himself floundering as he searched for something less provocative to say.

'Anyway, you might need to stand the bottle in some cold water before you open it. With a bit of luck it will cool the wine down enough to make it palatable.'

'I have one of those sleeves in the freezer that you put round wine bottles to chill them,' she informed him haughtily as she marched towards the kitchen door.

Ben groaned as he sank down onto the sofa. What was that saying about the road to hell and good intentions? He'd completely forgotten that they'd often resorted to chilling the cheap bottles of wine they'd bought from the supermarket by standing them in a bucket of cold water because the fridge in their flat had been so tiny that they'd not been able to fit a wine bottle into it. He hadn't thought about that for ages but his subconscious must have dredged up the memory. Holly obviously hadn't appreciated the reminder even though he hadn't intentionally tried to jog her memory. It was just so difficult to remember what was off limits. The twelve months they'd spent together had been the most important time of his entire life and he still tended to measure every experience by them.

'Can you get the cork out of this bottle for me? I seem to have split it.'

Ben's lips clamped together when he looked up and found Holly standing by the sofa with the bottle of wine in her hands. There was no way he was going to compound his errors by mentioning that she'd always been hopeless at opening wine bottles, he promised himself. He concentrated on digging out the cork but in the event it was Holly who broke the rules this time.

'I've always been *useless* at opening wine bottles. I can't count the number of times you had to fish out the cork after I'd smashed it to smithereens.'

'They can be tricky at times,' Ben observed through clenched teeth because he was terrified of making another blunder.

'They can, or at least they can for *me*.' She suddenly grinned. 'Do you remember that night your parents came round to the flat for dinner? We'd not long moved in and decided we'd ask them for a meal.'

Ben nodded because he didn't trust himself to speak. He remembered the night only too clearly. After his parents had left, he and Holly had made love in the sitting-room and afterwards he had asked her to marry him. It had been just one short week before his life had fallen apart...

'You were held up at work so I decided in my wisdom to open the wine myself and somehow managed to not only split the cork but also push it right down inside the bottle. We had to use a tea-strainer when we poured the wine to get all the bits out!'

Ben jumped when she laughed and the corkscrew bounced off the cork and embedded itself into the back of his left hand. He swore under his breath as he put the bottle on the floor and hunted in his pocket for a handkerchief to stem the blood that was gushing from the cut.

'What have you done? Let me see.' Holly knelt beside him, tutting in dismay when she saw his hand. 'That corkscrew has taken a real chunk out of you. Sit there while I find something to put on it.'

'It's fine,' he began, but he may as well have saved his breath because she was already on her way out of the room.

He sighed as he sank back against the cushions. If he'd believed in omens, they certainly wouldn't have boded well for the rest of the evening. It was an effort to appear outwardly calm when Holly came back with a box of adhesive dressings and some antiseptic wipes.

'We'd better make sure that cut is clean before we put a dressing on it,' she said, crouching down in front of him. She tore open a wipe and cleaned his hand, pausing when he winced. 'Sorry. Does that hurt?'

'Yes, but I'll try to be brave,' he told her, aiming for levity because it was better than letting her see how he really felt. The touch of her fingers on his skin had set up a chain reaction and cells which had had no contact for years were suddenly sending messages to each other. He sucked in his breath when the first of those signals arrived at one particular part of his body he would have preferred not to think about right then.

'That's the spirit,' she said encouragingly. She finished cleaning the cut then found an adhesive dressing and stuck it into place. 'There. That should do the trick.'

'Thanks,' Ben murmured distractedly, because it was alarming how quickly he had responded to her when he'd been so determined to keep a level head. Just the feel of her fingers on his skin had made his blood heat and his body start clamouring for lots more attention. He worked up a smile, hoping and praying that she couldn't tell how confused he felt.

'I must remember to have a box of plasters at the ready the next time I open a bottle of wine. It will save me dripping blood all over the place.'

'These things happen,' she replied lightly, dropping the bits into the waste-paper bin.

'I suppose so.' He quickly filled their glasses with wine, deeming it wiser to get back on track as fast as he could. 'Here you are. Let's just hope it was worth all the fuss in the end.'

'I'm sure it will be fine.' She accepted a glass of the wine and put it on the coffee-table then sat down and looked at him steadily. 'Look, Ben, there's no point beating around the bush. I asked you here to-night because there are some questions I want to ask you. But before we go any further, I want you to promise me something.'

Ben felt his insides churn because he had no idea what she was going to ask him. 'And that is?'

'That you'll tell me the truth no matter how…how difficult it is.'

His heart spasmed when he heard the quaver in her voice. It was obvious that Holly was worried about what he might tell her and it hurt to know that she was suffering such torment. 'I promise that I'll be as honest as I can,' he said, knowing that it wasn't quite what she'd been wanting from him.

'If that's the best you can do then I suppose I'll just have to accept it.'

She got up and went to the window then stood there with her back towards him. Ben guessed that she found it easier not to look at him and was suddenly consumed with guilt. He had hurt her such a lot and even though it had been the last thing he'd intended to do, he would never be able to forgive himself for what he'd done.

'Two years ago you told me that you'd met someone else and that was why you wanted us to split up.'

'That's right,' he agreed hoarsely, because he had a horrible feeling that he knew where this was leading.

'In that case, can you explain when you found the time to see her?'

She swung round and his heart sank when he saw the determination in her eyes. It was obvious that she wouldn't let him fob her off with some story yet he had no idea what he was going to tell her. It was hard to remain calm when she continued.

'I've tried to work it out, Ben, but I simply cannot understand how you managed to carry on an affair while we were living together. We were both working such crazy hours and what little free time we had, we spent it together. Either you discovered some miraculous way of adding extra hours to each day or you were lying and there was no other woman. So,

which was it? Was there someone else? Or did you
just use that as an excuse to end our relationship?'

Holly could feel her heart racing. She knew it was a
risk to ask him a question like that but she had no
choice. She had to get to the bottom of this mystery
before it drove her completely crazy.

'I really can't see any point in this, Holly,' he
began, but she didn't let him finish.

'The *point* is that I need to know the truth.' She
shrugged, praying that he couldn't tell how important
this was to her. She'd spent the time since she'd got
home from work going over and over every single
day they'd spent together and, no matter how hard
she'd tried, she still couldn't work out how Ben had
found the time to carry on an affair. That meant he'd
been lying to her and that he'd had another reason
for wanting them to split up. It was what that reason
might have been which was so important.

'I know it won't change what happened, Ben, but
I think I deserve to know if you were telling me a
pack of lies.'

'Look, Holly, I never wanted to hurt you. You
have to believe that!'

Her heart ached when she heard the anguish in his
voice but she couldn't afford to weaken at this stage.
'I'm not disputing that. I just want to know the truth.
Did you have an affair while we were living together?'

'No.' He put his head in his hands and she heard
him groan. 'You're quite right, Holly, because there

wasn't enough time for me to have had an affair even if I'd wanted to!'

And he hadn't wanted to?

Just for a second hope flared before she ruthlessly stamped it down. She couldn't afford to get side-tracked. She had to stick to her objective and make him tell her what his real reasons had been for ending their relationship. At the time everything had seemed so perfect that it had come like a bolt from the blue when Ben had announced that he was leaving her. Something had to have happened to have made him do that and she needed to know what it was.

'Then, if you didn't leave me for another woman, why did you leave me? Did you grow tired of me? Did you find our sex life boring or what?' Her voice rose and she had to breathe deeply before she could continue. 'You must have had a very good reason, Ben, and I want to know what it was.'

'It just wasn't going to work, Holly. I realised that and decided it would be better if we split up. Why can't you just leave it at that?'

She heard the impatience in his voice but it was tinged with sadness and it was that which made a mockery of what he was saying. If Ben regretted their parting then why had he been the one to insti-gate it?

'Because it doesn't make sense! That's why. I could understand you wanting to leave me if there was someone else involved, but to now claim that our relationship wouldn't have worked is absolute rubbish!' She glared at him as he stood up and crossed the room. 'You'd asked me to *marry* you,

Ben, and now you're saying that you suddenly realised we weren't suited?'

'Yes, that's it exactly! I had second thoughts and decided it would be best if we split up. I told you that I'd met someone else because I thought it might make it easier for you.'

'Easier?' She laughed, scarcely able to believe what she was hearing. 'I was making plans for our wedding when you suddenly announced that you'd met someone else, and you really think that it made the situation *easier* for me?'

'No, of course not. I didn't mean it that way....' he began, but all of a sudden Holly knew that she didn't want to hear any more.

'It doesn't matter. Forget it. You've answered my question and that's all I wanted.' She tried to push past him but he caught hold of her arm and brought her to a halt.

'Look, Holly, I know I made an unholy mess of things but I swear that I never intended to hurt you.'

'So you said.'

She stared pointedly at his hand but he still didn't release her and a shiver danced through her as she suddenly became aware of just how warm his fingers felt. She could feel their heat searing her flesh and maybe it was that which stopped her wrenching her arm away—that, plus the memory of all the other times Ben had held her, touched her.

'I meant it, too. I thought the world of you, Holly. Hurting you wasn't an option but I had no choice at the time. It was the best possible thing I could do, believe me.'

His hand slowly slid down her arm until it came to rest on her wrist and Holly's breath caught when she felt his thumb grazing her pulse. She knew he would feel how rapidly it was beating but there was nothing she could do about it. Her eyes rose to his face and she was shocked when she saw the yearning in his eyes. Why was he looking at her like that? Why was he staring at her as though he still cared when everything that had happened proved otherwise?

She ached to ask him but before she could find the right words his head suddenly dipped and all rational thoughts fled the moment his lips touched hers. He kissed her softly and with great tenderness then drew back to look at her and what he saw on her face must have convinced him to carry on. This time his mouth was more demanding, his lips seeking a response she was powerless to refuse. This was Ben who was holding her, Ben whose lips were working their magic, Ben who knew exactly how to arouse her hunger.

Holly wrapped her arms around his neck as passion flared between them and drew his head down so that she could kiss him back. They'd always been equal partners in bed and nothing had changed in that respect at least. Ben was as happy to let her lead as he was to have her follow, and she led him now, opening her mouth to tease his lips with the tip of her tongue, letting it slide inside his mouth and tangle with his in a ritual as old as time.

He gasped as he pulled away. 'Have you any idea what you're doing to me, Holly?' he demanded.

'Yes. Why d'you think I did it?' she murmured, looking straight into his eyes.

'Wicked woman!' His laughter was deep and sexy as he pulled her against him so that she could feel his body pulsing against hers. 'Don't you have any compassion at all?'

'Tons. That's why I don't intend to let you go until we...*solve* your dilemma.'

'I don't think that would be a good idea, Holly,' he warned, his voice throbbing with need.

'I think it's the perfect idea,' she countered. She held his gaze, wanting there to be no doubt about what she was saying. 'We both need to exorcise a few ghosts, Ben. Once that's done then we'll be able to put the past behind us for good.'

'Do you really think that making love would help us to do that?' he said sceptically, so sceptically, in fact, that she almost wavered.

However, in her heart she knew that she would never be free until she'd cut all the ties that bound them. She'd not had a real relationship with a man since they had split up. Something had always held her back but if she could view sex with Ben as a purely physical act and no longer as part of a committed relationship then she would be able to move on.

'Yes, I do, although I can't force you to have sex with me if it isn't what you want.' She felt him wince at the use of the word 'sex' but he didn't correct her and she was glad about that. If this was to work then they both needed to maintain a certain degree of detachment.

'I don't think you'll need to force me, Holly. Just so long as you're sure that you know what you're doing…?'

He left the question open and she answered it the best way she knew. His gasp was echoed by hers as their mouths joined in a kiss that was pure fire. When it was over she took his hand and led him into her bedroom, closing the door before she turned to him. She unzipped her trousers and stepped out of them then shed her T-shirt and underwear so that she was naked.

Ben's eyes travelled the full length of her body before they came back to her face. 'Are you sure about this, Holly? Absolutely certain it's what you want?'

'Yes. I'm sure.'

She held out her arms, her breath catching when he took hold of her and held her tightly against him. She could feel his heart beating beneath her breast and the pounding it made was proof of how important this was to him, too. Maybe Ben needed this as much as she did to bring their relationship to an end.

It was a bitter-sweet thought and she was glad when she didn't have time to dwell on it. Ben's hands were already working their magic and she gasped when she felt him cupping her breasts then cried out when he bent and suckled her nipples. Her legs suddenly buckled and she would have fallen if he hadn't picked her up in his arms and carried her to the bed.

He gently laid her down then shed his clothes and lay down beside her. Holly let her hands roam over him, relearning all the once-familiar curves and hollows—only there were a lot more hollows than there had been before because he'd lost so much weight. She longed to ask him what had happened but she knew it would be a mistake. This was an ending, not a beginning, and there was no point asking questions.

Tears welled to her eyes at that thought but she blinked them away. She wouldn't cry, certainly wouldn't have regrets later. She'd made her decision and no matter what happened she wasn't going back on it. They would have this one last night together and then, finally, it would be over between them and they could go on from there, build a new relationship as colleagues instead of lovers.

She turned into his arms and held him tightly as passion swept them away and if it took them to places they had never been before then she didn't let herself think about that either. This wasn't the first of many such occasions to come but the last of many that had gone before. This was just sex with Ben, a way to slake a physical need and set each other free even if her foolish mind kept trying to think of it as something more. This really and truly was the end of their affair.

CHAPTER SEVEN

'HE's arrested! We'll need to defib him again.'

Ben quickly applied the defibrillator's paddles to the man's chest while Holly set the dials to the correct voltage. It was the second time the patient had arrested since they'd got there and he mentally crossed his fingers that they would be able to get him back again.

'Clear!' Ben watched the man's body arch as the electric current passed through him, thinking what a crazy way this was to earn a living. He'd only just arrived at work that morning when the first call had come in. A farmer had suffered a heart attack on a farm high up in the hills surrounding Dalverston and the rapid response unit had been asked to attend because of the difficulties of getting an ambulance there. He and Holly had used the four-wheel-drive vehicle again to get to the farm, travelling along a series of increasingly rough tracks. The farmer—a man in his fifties called Denis Anderson—had been conscious when they'd arrived but he'd suffered a second heart attack whilst they'd been examining him. Now it was in the lap of the gods whether they would be able to drag him back from the brink once more.

'Sinus rhythm,' Holly announced.

'Thank heavens!' Ben heaved a sigh of relief because he really couldn't face losing a patient this early in the day. 'Let's get him into the car before he goes down again. The sooner we get him to hospital, the happier I'll be.'

'You don't think we should call for an ambulance?' Holly queried, quickly repacking the Thomas pack.

'It'll be faster if we take him ourselves. It could take an hour or more for an ambulance to get here and the next time he goes down we might not be so lucky,' Ben explained, marvelling at the fact that they were both behaving so calmly after what had happened the night before.

He sighed as Holly went to tell to Denis's wife what they were doing. He still couldn't believe they'd ended up in bed together. Holly had been so certain it had been what she'd wanted but he couldn't help wondering if it had been a mistake for him. Making love to Holly had aroused a lot of feelings he'd tried to bury in the past two years. It hadn't been easy to let her go but he'd always felt it had been the right thing to do. However, last night had simply highlighted how much he had lost. Maybe *she* believed it had drawn a line under the past but it could never be that simple for him.

'Denis's wife wants to know if she can come with us. She doesn't drive and won't be able to get to the hospital if we can't take her.'

Ben switched his thoughts back to professional mode as Holly came back. 'It will be a bit of squeeze but we should be able to fit her in. How will she get back here, though?'

'Apparently, her son is going to meet her at the hospital and he'll bring her home.'

'So long as you're happy then it's fine by me,' Ben agreed readily, fastening the last strap on the stretcher and standing up. 'I'll back the car over here to save us having to wheel Denis over all those ruts.'

'I'll do it,' Holly offered, holding out her hand for the keys. 'You drove here so I'll drive back.'

'Fair enough.'

Ben didn't argue as he handed over the car keys then checked that they'd got everything. Their equipment was very costly and he would hate to leave any of it behind. Denis's wife came running out of the farmhouse, clutching a small canvas holdall, and he smiled at her. 'I see you've managed to pack a bag for your husband.'

'Just some clean pyjamas and his shaving things.' Tears suddenly began to trickle down the woman's face. 'Although I don't know if he'll need them. He's going to die, isn't he?'

'Not if we have anything to do with it,' Ben assured her. 'We've managed to get his heart back into its proper rhythm and we've given him drugs to dissolve any blood clots. If we can get him back to the coronary care unit, he stands a very good chance of recovering.'

'But will he be able to work again?' June Anderson persisted. 'My dad had a heart attack, you see, and he was never the same afterwards. He spent the rest of his life sitting in a chair and Denis would hate that. This farm is his whole life and I don't know what he'll do if he can't carry on working.'

'It's far too early to say whether or not he'll be fit to work,' Ben explained patiently. He glanced round as Holly drew up beside them. 'Let's just concentrate on getting your husband to hospital, shall we? That's the most important thing at the moment.'

June nodded but Ben could tell how upset she was. He sighed as he helped to manoeuvre the stretcher into the vehicle. As he knew to his own cost, the effects of any serious illness had far-reaching consequences for everyone concerned.

'Ambulance Control has just been on the radio to ask if they should send an ambulance to meet us on the bypass,' Holly told him as they all climbed into the front. 'I told them we'd take the patient directly to hospital ourselves.'

'That's fine,' Ben agreed. 'There's no point tying up an ambulance as well. Right, everything's sorted so let's get a move on.'

'Wagons roll!' she replied cheerily.

Ben fastened his seat belt as she started the engine. It was a bit of a squeeze with June squashed in the middle but they could hardly have left the poor woman behind. He glanced at Holly as they set off and frowned when she gave him a carefree smile in return. She seemed completely at ease so could he take it that last night's experiment had had the desired results? Did she now feel that she could put the past behind her and get on with living life to the full?

He turned and stared through the window because that thought aroused a wealth of conflicting emotions. He was glad that Holly was happy, of course, but a part of him—a part he didn't like very much—

hated the thought of her making plans that didn't include him. If he'd learned anything from last night, it was the fact that he wasn't over her.

Not by a long chalk.

'You'll be able to see Denis as soon as they've got him settled into the coronary care unit. He's in good hands, June, so try not to worry.'

Holly managed to hold her smile while the woman thanked her again for all that she'd done, but it was a relief when she was able to make her escape. She went straight to the staffroom and plugged in the kettle, hoping she would have time for a cup of coffee before she was needed again. She hadn't bothered with any breakfast that morning so it was little wonder that she was feeling so jittery.

She grimaced as she spooned instant coffee into a mug. There was no point pretending her jumpiness was the result of low blood sugar. The strain of trying to behave as though everything was fine was the real cause of her problems. What on earth had possessed her to sleep with Ben last night? At the time it had seemed to make a lot of sense but she'd quickly realised afterwards what a mistake it had been. Far from bringing the past to its rightful conclusion, it had reawakened a lot of painful memories. It was hard to deal with the thought that she was going to have to learn to live without Ben all over again.

'Aha, you've beaten me to it, I see.'

Holly spun round when she heard Ben's voice. She had managed to behave with an outward semblance of calm while they'd been attending to Denis

Anderson. The man had been so ill that she'd been able to focus on the task of keeping him alive. However, the prospect of chatting with Ben over a cup of coffee after what had happened last night made her stomach start to churn.

'Do you want a cup of coffee?' she asked, hoping he couldn't tell how nervous she felt.

'Please.' He sank down onto a chair and groaned. 'What a start to the day! It was pretty hairy at times, wasn't it?'

'It was,' she agreed, adding milk and two spoons of sugar to one of the mugs. She gave Ben the mug then leant against the sink while she drank her own coffee because there was no way that she was going to risk sitting next to him while her emotions were in such turmoil.

'Mmm, I really need this.' He took an appreciative sip of the drink then grinned at her. 'Just the way I like it, too.'

Holly flushed when she realised that she'd automatically added both milk and sugar to his coffee. She hadn't needed to ask because she knew that Ben liked his coffee white and sweet, just as she knew that he liked his steak rare. All the little details that came from living together had been stored in her memory bank, ready to pop out the moment she needed them. It just seemed to prove what a fool she'd been to imagine she was over him.

'Sorry. Was that the wrong thing to say again?'

She looked up with a frown. 'Pardon?'

'Shouldn't I have mentioned that you know how I like my coffee?' He sighed heavily. 'To be honest,

Holly, it's really difficult to know what's on and what's off limits. I always seem to end up by putting my foot in it whenever we talk.'

'I shouldn't worry too much,' she said lightly, because she didn't want him making an issue out of it. 'We can't ignore the fact that we used to know each other extremely well.'

'Not just *used to* either. Not after last night.'

'Last night was a one-off and you know why it happened,' she countered, her heart hammering because it wasn't easy to talk about what they'd done.

'Meaning there's not going to be a repeat performance?'

'No. I made that clear at the time. I…I just wanted to draw a line under the past. That's all.'

'Then let's hope it worked.' He gave her a tight smile then downed his coffee in a single gulp and stood up. 'Anyway, I'd better get a move on. Sean has arranged for me to go out with Nicky and Josh today. Apparently, you all spent a day on the road with the paramedics during your training and Sean wants to bring me up to speed. I'll see you later…always assuming I survive, of course!'

'I'm sure Nicky will take good care of you,' she responded, adopting a deliberately upbeat tone.

She carried on drinking her coffee after he left but for some reason it tasted horribly bitter all of a sudden. She tipped it down the sink and rinsed her mug then fetched Ben's mug to wash it as well. There was some coffee still left in the bottom and on a sudden impulse she drank it. It tasted deliciously sweet after her own drink and she savoured it for a moment before it struck her that her lips were touching the exact same spot that Ben's had touched just moments before.

Holly closed her eyes, feeling the tremor that was working its way through her body as she recalled how Ben's lips had felt the previous night. He'd always been a wonderfully tender lover but last night they had seemed to reach new heights together. Every touch of his hands had been a delight, every kiss a blessing, and when they had finally joined....

'RTA on its way!' Lara announced, bursting into the staffroom.

Holly jumped as she was rudely brought back to earth with a bump and she saw Lara grimace.

'Sorry! I didn't mean to startle you. It's just that Sean's in Resus and Ben's gone swanning off so everyone's in a mad panic out there.'

'Don't worry. It was my own fault for standing here daydreaming,' Holly explained rather shakily as she put the cup in the sink.

'Oh, I *see*! I wonder what you were daydreaming about. It wouldn't have anything to do with a tall, dark, handsome specialist registrar, by any chance?' Lara grinned at her. 'And before you deny it, Holly, I should warn you that I've heard all about Ben following you into the ladies' loo the other day.'

Lara's face was a picture of curiosity but there was no way that Holly was going to admit that she *had* been thinking about Ben. 'I'll go and wait for the ambulance to arrive,' she told the young nurse with as much dignity as she could muster. 'Warn Sean that I'll be bringing another patient into Resus, will you?'

'Will do.'

Lara must have realised there was no point pursuing the subject and didn't say anything else before she hurried away. However, Holly knew it wouldn't be as easy to stop the gossip that was already circulating and sighed as she made her way to the ambulance bay. She could do without folk speculating about her and Ben. Maybe it was time to nip this in the bud by giving them something else to talk about? Josh was off duty that night so she could ask him if he fancied going for a pizza after work. It should put a stop to any rumours about her and Ben, even though she felt a bit mean about using Josh that way…although there was no reason why Josh should be just a decoy, of course. There was nothing to stop her going out with him for real if she wanted to. In fact, it might be the best thing to do because it would show Ben that she'd meant what she'd said about last night being a one-off, never-to-be-repeated experience. If there was someone else on the scene then Ben would *have* to believe she'd meant it.

As it turned out, Holly didn't get a chance to speak to Josh until almost the end of her shift. Although the paramedics were in and out of the A and E department all day long, they were all far too busy to chat. It wasn't until she was asked to attend an accident at Dalverston Lake that she found the right moment to broach the subject.

Once again she used the motorbike to respond to the call. The evening rush hour was under way but the satellite navigation system helped her find a back route so she got to the lake in very good time. A small crowd of teenagers was gathered on the shore when she arrived and Holly hurried straight over to them, kneeling down on the shingle while she examined the boy. He'd been on a canoeing expedition organised by the local high school and had hit his head on a rock when his canoe had rolled over. Fortunately, the teacher in charge of the group had basic first-aid skills so he'd been able to give the boy CPR.

'How long was he underwater?' Holly asked, checking the boy's pulse. It was very faint and thready but at least he had a pulse.

'About two minutes. A couple of the other lads dived in and managed to turn his canoe over,' the teacher explained anxiously.

'Was he breathing when you got him ashore?' Holly continued, checking the boy's eyes. His right pupil was fixed and dilated—a sign that he had suffered a head injury.

'Not at first but I managed to start him breathing on his own again after about five minutes or so.'

'Well done! It isn't easy to put the theory into practice and not everyone can do it when the time comes.'

'I wasn't sure if I was doing it right,' the man admitted. 'It's rather different when you practise on one of those dummies that have a light attached to them. There was no green light to tell me if Mike was getting any of the oxygen I was trying to pump into him!'

'It's a shame we don't all have one of those little lights but you did extremely well without it.' Holly laughed as she deftly fitted the boy with a cervical collar to protect his neck. She looked round when she heard a siren. 'Here's the ambulance. We'll take him straight back to the hospital so can you let his parents know that's where he'll be. He's suffered a head injury from the look of it so we'll need to get a CT scan done as soon as we get him there.'

'He will be all right, though?' the teacher demanded anxiously.

'Let's hope so.'

Holly didn't say anything else because it wasn't possible to give a definite answer at that stage. She got up when Josh and Ben appeared with a stretcher. Nicky was backing the ambulance onto the shore so they moved the boy onto the stretcher and strapped him in.

'I'll meet you back at the hospital,' Holly told them. 'He needs a CT scan so I'll get it organised ready for when you arrive. He'll probably need surgery, too, so I'll warn Max to stand by.'

'Thanks.' Ben grabbed one end of the stretcher while Josh took the other and between them they managed to carry the teenager over the shingle and load him into the ambulance. Nicky opted to ride in the back with the boy so Ben closed the rear doors.

'We'll see you later,' he said, turning to Holly. 'Drive carefully.'

'I always do,' she replied lightly, because she didn't want him to guess how much the words had touched her....

She took a deep breath because she had to stop this nonsense. If Ben had *really* cared about her, he would never have left her. Her heart felt like lead as she turned to Josh but she knew it was the best thing to do.

'Do you fancy going out for a pizza after work tonight?'

'I'd love to!' Josh replied eagerly. 'I'll meet you in the staff car park after we finish. OK?'

'Fine.' Holly avoided looking at Ben as the two men climbed into the cab. However, she couldn't help noticing that, although Josh waved as they drove away, Ben didn't even glance at her.

She sighed as she went back to the motorbike. If Ben had a problem about her seeing Josh then it was up to him to deal with it. She'd made it perfectly clear that last night had been just a means to an end so there was no reason for her to feel guilty because she was going out with someone else…

Only she couldn't help it. It felt as though she was letting Ben down and the idea scared her. How could she *hope* to make this work if she couldn't free herself from the ties that still bound her to Ben?

It was after seven by the time Ben got home that night. It was his own fault because he'd hung around waiting for news of Mike Parker, the boy who'd been injured in the canoeing accident. The CT scans had shown a subdural haemorrhage—bleeding into the space between the outer and middle layers of tissue that covered the brain—and Max had decided to operate to remove the blood clot. Thankfully, the operation had gone well and Ben had been able to break the good news to Mike's parents before he'd left. It had been the one bright spot at the end of what had turned out to be an extremely stressful day.

He let himself into the flat and sank down on the bed. He felt completely worn out and it wasn't just because the day had been so hectic either. How on earth was he expected to deal with the thought of Holly spending the evening with Josh when *he* wanted to be the one taking her out for a pizza, the one seeing her home afterwards, the one who would be invited in for coffee and…

'Hell!' He shot to his feet. He would drive himself crazy if he sat there all night thinking things like that. He needed to *do* something to take his mind off what might be happening. He'd passed the cinema on his way home so he'd go there and watch a film.

He chose an all-action thriller but the plot was so ludicrous that it failed to hold his attention. His mind kept drifting this way and that, always coming back to the one subject guaranteed to cause him grief: Holly and Josh. In the end, Ben admitted defeat and left. Nothing was going to stop him thinking about Holly so he may as well go home.

He bought fish and chips on the way and ate them out of the paper. It was a beautiful night, a bright silvery moon lighting up the whole town. It seemed a shame to spend the evening in the cramped confines of his bedsit so he carried on walking and ended up at a park close to the river. There was a children's playground sectioned off from the main area so he sat on one of the swings while he finished his supper.

He still didn't feel like going home after he'd eaten the last chip, mainly because there was nobody to go home to. And that thought, naturally, led him right back to where he'd started. Holly.

He took a deep breath because there was no point lying to himself. He was still in love with Holly. Now that he'd admitted it, he needed to take steps to ensure she never found out and the best way of doing that was by accepting that she had her own life to lead. He mustn't say or do anything to make her suspect how he felt about her seeing Josh. It wouldn't be fair. He'd ruined her life once already and he wasn't going to ruin it a second time.

He tossed the chip paper into the bin and stood up. He either had to learn to live with the situation or he would have to leave Dalverston, and he couldn't face the thought of cutting himself off completely. Maybe he *could* only watch over Holly from the sidelines from now on but it would be better than nothing.

CHAPTER EIGHT

'So HOW was your evening? You shot out of the flat
so fast this morning that I never got the chance to
ask. Although, from the smile on Josh's face, I'd
hazard a guess that it went extremely well!'

Holly bit back a sigh when Nicky waylaid her in
the corridor as she was coming out of the treatment
room. She'd left home early that morning to avoid
any awkward questions, but it had soon become apparent that it had been a waste of time. It wasn't just
Nicky who was interested in her date with Josh—the
whole *department* seemed to know that she'd been
out with him and she'd done nothing but field questions ever since she'd arrived at work. Her little ploy
to divert attention away from her and Ben had been
remarkably successful, in fact.

'It was fine, thank you very much,' she replied,
trying to control the pang of guilt that assailed her
again. Even though nothing had happened, apart
from her spending a pleasant couple of hours with
Josh, it still felt as though she'd done something
wrong.

'Great! So when are you going out with him
again?' Nicky fell into step beside her. 'I tried prising
all the gory details out of Josh but he was like the
proverbial clam and wouldn't tell me a thing.'

'That's because there's nothing to tell,' Holly retorted tartly, taking a file out of the tray. It had been another busy morning and the information board above the Reception desk was warning people there would be a two-hour delay before they could be seen.

'You mean he didn't ask you out again!' Nicky exclaimed in dismay. 'I shall have to have a serious word with him. Fancy letting an opportunity like that slip through his fingers…'

'We're probably going to the cinema next week,' Holly put in quickly, because she knew what Nicky was like once she got a bee in her bonnet. 'Josh needs to check when he's working before we can make any definite arrangements. Sean's altering the shifts because he's taken on another paramedic and he wants Josh to supervise the new man for a few days.'

'Oh, I see!' Nicky beamed with delight. 'You had me worried for a moment. I think it's really brilliant that you two have got together at last. Josh has been driving me mad, going on and on about how gorgeous you are. The poor guy's totally smitten.'

'Is he?' Holly summoned a smile but her stomach had sunk on hearing that. She liked Josh but she knew in her heart that they would never be anything more than friends. There simply wasn't that kind of a spark between them, and definitely nothing that resembled the attraction she'd felt for Ben.

'Uh-huh. I told you I could hear wedding bells, didn't I?'

'Then I'm afraid your hearing must be faulty.' Holly knew her friend was only teasing but she hated to think that Josh might get the wrong idea if he overheard comments like that. 'I like Josh but the truth is that I'm not interested in a long-term relationship at the moment.'

'Oh, dear.' Nicky grimaced. 'I'm really sorry, Holly. I didn't mean to cause any problems.'

'What do you mean?' Holly demanded when she saw the stricken expression on Nicky's face.

'Just that I might have, well…*hinted* to Josh that you were rather keen on him, too.'

'You didn't?' She sighed when Nicky nodded. 'Why on earth did you do something so stupid?'

'Because I hate seeing Josh looking so fed up. He was getting very downhearted because you never seemed to notice him.'

'That's all well and good but I wish you hadn't said anything,' she protested. 'I know you meant well, Nicky, but it's not fair on Josh. He's just a friend and that's all he'll ever be, I'm afraid.'

'I'm really sorry, Holly. Maybe I should have another word with him and explain that I got it wrong,' Nicky offered, but Holly shook her head.

'No, just leave things as they are. Josh will only be embarrassed if you say anything and I certainly don't want to make things awkward when we have to work together.'

She glanced round when the office phone rang. When Sean appeared and beckoned to her it was a relief because she really didn't want to continue the conversation. If she'd realised the problems it was going to cause then she would *never* have suggested to Josh that they go out for that pizza.

'That's me out of here,' she said, dropping the file back into the tray. 'I'll see you later.'

'Yep. And I really am sorry, Holly. Next time I'll keep my big mouth shut!'

Holly didn't reply as she hurried along the corridor. With a bit of luck it would all blow over in a few days although she would need to rethink her plans about seeing Josh again. It wouldn't be fair to lead him on when nothing would come of it.

She grimaced because there was no point pretending why she was so sure that she and Josh didn't have a future together. It was all down to Ben and to the fact that she couldn't imagine loving any man again the way she'd loved him. She had to get over it, though. Ben Carlisle couldn't be the only man on the planet who could make her hormones run riot!

Sean was on the phone when she reached the office and he waved her towards a chair. He must have summoned Ben as well because he arrived a few seconds later and sat down next to her while they waited for Sean to finish his call.

'We've got a light aircraft that's crashed in woodland close to the motorway,' Sean explained as he hung up. 'Ambulance Control has no idea how many casualties but they want us to respond. They'll be sending ambulances once they know exactly what we're dealing with.'

'What's the access to the site like?' Ben asked, frowning.

'Not good from what I can gather, which is why they've asked us to attend. You'll need to use the four-wheel-drive. Apparently, the plane came down in the middle of the woods so the police are going to meet you at the motorway junction and show you the way from there. I'm not sure what you're going to find but there's bound to be a lot of high-octane aviation fuel about so you'll need to be extremely careful what you're doing.'

'We'll be fine,' Holly assured him. 'We won't take any risks.'

'Make sure you don't!' he warned.

She and Ben left the office together, stopping *en route* to collect their equipment. Holly wriggled into the bright green suit and zipped it up then pulled on a fluorescent yellow vest emblazoned with the word DOCTOR across the back. A lightweight safety helmet came next and then she was ready to leave.

'What about your boots?' Ben looked pointedly at her feet. 'You can't go tramping about in the wood in those.'

'Drat! I forgot. I'd better change them.' She grabbed her boots off the shelf and sat down on the bench to change out of the comfortable shoes she wore around the hospital.

'Here you go.' Ben crouched in front of her and pulled the leather tongue out of the left boot to loosen the laces.

'Thanks, but I can manage,' she protested, trying to take the boot from him.

'It isn't a problem,' he assured her, his fingers cupping her heel as he lifted her foot off the floor and guided it into the boot.

Holly bit her lip as a rush of heat spread from her foot and raced up her leg. She quickly slid her right foot into the other boot before he could help her and laced them both up. Ben was waiting by the door when she finished and she summoned a carefree smile as she joined him.

'Good practice for when you next play Prince Charming, eh?'

'Something like that,' he replied rather gruffly.

Holly shot him a wary look as they let themselves into the garage. Had he been annoyed by that flippant remark or was there something else bothering him? She sighed as she opened the car door and climbed into the passenger seat because once again she was falling into the trap of worrying how Ben felt. She had to remember to distance herself, keep it in mind that they were colleagues now instead of partners.

She carefully kept that thought in the forefront of her mind as Ben drove away from the hospital. Although she'd never attended a plane crash before, she'd read about the types of injuries they might encounter. Crush injuries would be one of their main problems, along with multiple fractures. Then there could be open wounds plus burns if the plane had caught fire. She and Ben could find themselves dealing with any or all of those and it was a little bit scary as well as exciting to think about what lay ahead.

'Ever been to a plane crash before?' Ben suddenly asked.

'No, never. How about you?'

'Me neither.' He turned and grinned at her and she felt her heart kick in an extra beat when she saw the excitement in his eyes. 'Think we'll cope?'

'Of course,' she replied, trying to inject a note of firmness into her voice, no easy feat when her insides felt as though they were melting into mush. Ben's smile had always had the power to affect her and it was just as potent now as it had ever been.

'Mmm, good to hear you sounding so confident.'

'I wouldn't dare admit it even if I was scared stiff!' she countered pithily. 'You were the one who drummed it into me that I had to learn to trust my own judgement if I hoped to survive this type of work, don't forget.'

'Oh, I haven't forgotten. It's just that life has a nasty habit of knocking you back when you least expect it. Still, I'm glad to hear that you're feeling up to the challenge because it doesn't sound as though today's little incident is going to be a picnic.'

Holly frowned because there seemed to be more to that comment than had first appeared. Had *Ben's* confidence been rocked in the past couple of years by something that had happened to him?

It was hard to accept because he'd always been so sure of himself and his own ability. To imagine him suffering any kind of doubts simply didn't gel with the image she had of him. She shot him a careful look but he was concentrating on the traffic as they approached the motorway and she bit her lip in a quandary of indecision. She could ask him to explain, of course, but would it be wise to do that when just a few minutes ago she'd resolved to keep her distance?

It was hard to decide what to do and in the end she was forced to let the matter drop because they'd reached the slip road where the police were waiting for them. However, as Ben drew up to speak to an officer, she knew that she couldn't just forget what he'd said. If something had happened to rock Ben's legendary confidence then it had to be something really momentous. It was difficult enough to deal with that idea but even harder to cope with the one that followed it: had it been that event which had made him decide to end their relationship?

Holly's heart began to drum as they set off again because the thought that Ben might not have *wanted* them to split up if he'd had a choice had changed everything.

'We'll need to get them out of there. How long will it be before the fire brigade gets here?'

Ben waited while the police officer consulted his colleagues. They'd had to park the vehicles on the edge of the wood and travel the rest of the way on foot so they'd already lost a lot of valuable time. His main concern now was to get the passengers out of the plane so he and Holly could examine them but unfortunately the doors had jammed shut on impact. He shook his head when the policeman informed him that it would be another ten minutes before the fire crew arrived at the scene.

'That's far too long. We'll have to get them out of there ourselves.'

He turned to Holly, steeling himself when he saw the expression on her face. What on earth had possessed him to pass that comment? He'd realised immediately that she'd picked up on it and it had been sheer good luck that he'd not had to explain because he doubted if he could have come up with anything plausible. He'd have to be more careful in future. He certainly didn't want to tell her the truth at this stage when it would look as though he was trying to split up her and Josh by doling out some sort of a sob story.

'Can you get on to Ambulance Control and tell them that we have five casualties? Explain that we haven't been able to examine them yet but that we're going to need ambulances standing by to ferry them to hospital.'

'Will do.'

Holly took the radio out of their Thomas pack and moved away from the plane. He watched her press the call button a couple of times.

'Can't you get a signal?'

'No. It must be the trees.' She nodded her thanks when a policeman offered her his radio to use but the reception was no better on that. 'I'll try walking back up the path.' she explained. 'We passed a clearing on our way and I might be able to get a better signal there. Won't be long.'

'OK.' Ben turned his attention to the plane as she hurried away, wishing he didn't feel so relieved that he had some time on his own. He certainly wasn't making a very good job of dealing with this situation despite his earlier resolve. One of the police officers had had the foresight to bring along a crowbar and between them they managed to force open the cockpit door. Ben leant inside the cockpit but it didn't take him long to establish that the pilot was dead.

They lifted him out then Ben climbed in and checked the passengers next. Three were dead and the fourth, a man in his thirties, was in a very bad way. He shook his head when the police officer asked him how the man was.

'Alive. That's the best I can say. It's difficult to tell what injuries he's sustained until we get him out.' He broke off when he heard someone shouting, feeling his heart leap right into his throat when he recognised Holly's voice. He scrambled out of the plane and ran to meet her as she came racing out of the trees. 'What's happened?'

'I've found a child in the clearing. It looks as though the plane must have hit a tree as it was coming down and sheared off some of the branches. The boy's pinned beneath one of them and I can't tell how badly injured he is.'

'In that case, you'd better deal with him while I stay here. We've got four dead and one still alive, although it will be touch and go whether he survives.' Ben glanced round when he heard voices coming from the trees and sighed in relief when he saw the firemen heading towards them. 'Looks like the cavalry has arrived at last so we should be able to make some headway.'

'I'll get one of them to go with me and take a look at this branch,' Holly told him, hurrying away.

Ben ran back to the plane. The passenger was still alive but his vital signs weren't good. He did what he could—oxygen and fluids, analgesics to relieve any pain, plus a neck brace to guard against any fur-

ther damage when they lifted him out of the plane.
The officer in charge of the fire crew decided there
was too much fuel about to risk using the cutting
gear so they had to manoeuvre the man out through
the cockpit door and simply hope they wouldn't
make matters worse.

Ben checked him over again, feeling increasingly
despondent as he logged up injury after injury. There
was barely a bone in the poor fellow's body that
wasn't broken and Ben didn't rate his chances very
highly. However, he did everything he could then
passed him over to the paramedics and went to see
how Holly was faring. He found her lying on the
ground beside the child, talking to him while the firemen cut through the branch.

Ben ground to a halt, feeling his heart aching. It
was like a rerun of the first time he'd ever seen her
and the effect it had on him now was every bit as
potent. He loved her so much yet he could never tell
her that. Quite apart from the uncertainty of what the
future might hold in store for him, there was the fact
that the treatment he'd received for his cancer could
have done all kinds of damage.

His consultant had warned him at the outset that
the chemotherapy could leave him sterile and he'd
never had the guts or the desire to find out if it had.
He'd been offered the chance of having some of his
sperm frozen and had agreed to it because it had
seemed easier than arguing that there was no point.
Everyone had kept telling him that it was the right
thing to do and he simply hadn't had the heart to

explain that the only woman he'd ever wanted to
have his babies now hated him.

He closed his eyes as huge wave of pain ripped
through him. What a mess it all was, what a rotten,
horrible mess!

'Shh. You're going to be fine. Don't be scared now.
You just squeeze my hand and we'll soon have you
out of there.'

Holly winced as the boy gripped her fingers. She
glanced up to ask the firemen how much longer it
would take to free him but the question got all tan-
gled up in her throat when she suddenly spotted Ben
standing on the edge of the clearing. There was an
expression of such anguish on his face that her heart
turned over. Coming on top of what had happened
earlier, it was impossible to ignore it. No matter how
risky it was to get involved, she knew that she
wouldn't rest until she found out what had happened
to him.

The boy suddenly whimpered as the saw sliced
through the last section the branch and Holly
quickly turned her attention back to him as the firemen lifted the branch out of the way. She quickly
examined the boy but, amazingly, she couldn't find
any serious injuries. He had several nasty abra-
sions—one on his cheek and another on his arm
where a large strip of skin had been shaved away—
but she couldn't find evidence of even a single broken bone.

'How is he?'

Holly kept her gaze fixed on the child as Ben came

hurrying over and squatted down beside her. Maybe it was cowardly but she wasn't sure she'd be able to maintain her composure if he still looked upset. 'Much better than I feared. Take a look yourself because I can't find anything obviously wrong, apart from a few cuts and bruises, of course.'

She sat back on her heels and watched while Ben examined the boy. His hands moved systematically over the child, gently probing and testing his limbs, and a rush of heat assailed her as she recalled how those same hands had caressed her the other night. Despite their hunger for each other, Ben hadn't rushed: he'd taken his time as he'd brought her body to life, touching her in ways no other man had ever done. He'd seemed to derive as much pleasure from it as she had, in fact, and that thought was another one that came with a question tagged on the end: why should he have been so moved by the experience if he didn't still care about her?

'He looks OK to me, although obviously we'll need X-rays to confirm it,' he announced at last, looking up.

'Then let's get him to hospital.'

Holly quickly schooled her face into a neutral expression as she stood up. She certainly didn't want Ben to suspect what was going through her mind because she needed to find out the truth. Something told her that he would avoid giving her the answers she wanted if he could do so. The other night was a prime example of that, wasn't it? He'd told her nothing apart from the fact that he'd lied about his reasons for ending their relationship, but she wasn't going to let him get away again that easily a second time.

Ben went away to fetch the paramedics while Holly patched up the child's cuts. She kept him talking to take his mind off what she was doing and quickly discovered that his name was Daniel Harris, that he was twelve years old and lived with his parents on the other side of the woods. When Ben came back with the paramedics, she relayed the information to them and they promised to radio it through to base so that someone could go to the boy's home and tell his parents what had happened.

'Aren't you coming with me?' Daniel demanded, clinging tightly to her hand as the paramedics picked up the stretcher. 'I don't want to go on my own!'

'Yes, of course I'll come if you want me to,' Holly quickly assured him.

She turned to Ben, thinking that it might be a good idea if she travelled in the ambulance. Not only would it help to calm Daniel down but it would stop her being too premature and trying to cross-question Ben. Although she was desperate to hear what he had to say, she really needed to speak to him on his own, without any distractions. 'You don't mind if I go back in the ambulance, do you?'

'Of course not. I'll see you back at the hospital.'

There was a shade too much eagerness about the way he agreed to her request. Holly smiled rather grimly as she followed the paramedics along the path through the woods. Had Ben sensed something was going on? Her smile turned even grimmer because she was going to get to the bottom of this mystery. One way or the other!

It was way past the time she should have gone off duty when they arrived back at Dalverston General but Daniel pleaded with her to stay with him while his X-rays were taken and Holly didn't have the heart to refuse. Ben popped into Resus as she was waiting for the films to show up on the screen, and told her that he would write up their report before he left.

Holly politely thanked him, hoping he couldn't tell that her nerves were positively fizzing with impatience. This was neither the time nor the place to start a discussion but she promised herself that as soon as she'd finished then she would go straight round to Ben's flat and have it out with him. They were both off duty over the weekend and there was no way that she could wait until Monday.

The X-rays confirmed that Daniel hadn't broken any bones so Holly gave instructions that he could be discharged when his parents arrived. She moved him to a cubicle and left him in the care of one of the junior nurses, who happened to be the sister of one of his school friends. She was just about to leave at last when his parents arrived. They, quite naturally, were anxious to know what had happened so she ended up by taking them to the relatives' room and telling them the whole story, from start to finish, so it was gone seven by the time she could make her escape. She hurried to the staffroom for her bag, almost knocking Lara over in her haste to leave before anything else cropped up.

'That's OK,' Lara said cheerfully when she apologised. 'Everyone's in a rush tonight. I hope Ben managed to catch his train. There's a massive traffic jam on the bypass so fingers crossed that he didn't get caught up in it.'

'Ben's catching a train?' Holly exclaimed. 'Where to?'

'He's going to stay with his parents for a few days. Didn't he mention it to you?'

'No, he didn't.'

'Funny. Still, perhaps he thought you had more important things on your mind, like a certain paramedic I could mention?'

Lara grinned at her and left. Holly sighed as she opened her locker. She should never have invited Josh to go for that pizza because it had caused more problems than it had solved. As for Ben, well, if she'd had any inkling that he was planning on going away that night then she would have insisted on talking to him earlier. Now she would have to wait until he came back and the thought of spending the weekend in such a state of uncertainty was more than she could bear. She wanted to get this sorted out because if they could only resolve their differences they might be able to try again.

She gasped in dismay. Was that what she *really* wanted? To be with Ben again? Was that why she was so desperate to get to the bottom of this mystery? Yet if they did get back together, would she ever be able to trust him again? She'd given him her love and her trust once before and he'd let her down.

Badly. Could she really see herself being brave enough to risk everything a second time?

A knot of pain suddenly formed in her heart because she couldn't answer that question. It depended on so many other factors. She would have to wait and make up her mind after she'd spoken to Ben.

CHAPTER NINE

BEN spent the weekend at his parents' house, pretending that his life was fine and that he couldn't have been happier. He'd never been good at deceiving people so it was a strain, keeping up the act, but it was better than having to face Holly.

Maybe he'd misread the situation but he'd sensed that she'd had something on her mind when they'd attended that plane crash. He'd been so desperate to avoid any more difficult discussions that he'd phoned his mother as soon as he'd got back to the hospital and asked if he could go home for a visit. It had been sheer cowardice, to run away like that, but if it meant that he wouldn't end up ruining Holly's life by telling her the truth then it had been justified. Holly deserved someone better than him, someone who had a future to offer her and who could give her children.

He went into work at lunchtime on Monday. The new rosters had been drawn up so he and Holly would be working overlapping shifts until another registrar was hired. It should mean them not spending as much time together but, as it happened, she was the first person he saw when he entered the building. His heart bopped up and down a couple of dozen times when he spotted her walking towards him.

'Hi! How's it been this morning? Busy?' he asked

in a deliberately upbeat tone which, hopefully, would disguise all the other emotions he was feeling. An absence of two days wasn't long enough to have missed her, he told himself sternly. However, as his eyes greedily drank in the sight of her, it felt as though a lifetime had passed since he'd seen her last.

'So-so. Did you have a good time with your parents? Lara told me that you'd gone to visit them.'

Her tone was decidedly cool and Ben hid his grimace because he could tell she was put out because he hadn't mentioned his trip. 'It was fine. It's always nice to be fussed over,' he replied, deeming it wiser not to admit that it had been a spur-of-the-moment decision in case it gave rise to any awkward questions. He sighed inwardly, hating the fact that it felt as though he was tiptoeing over eggshells whenever they spoke.

'It is. Anyway, now that you're back, Ben, I was hoping we—'

'Oops, sorry. I'll have to go,' he cut in hastily. He stared past her, hoping that his acting abilities had improved during the past couple of days. 'I'm sure I saw Sean waving to me just now.'

'Really? You must have the most amazing eyesight, then, because Sean was in Resus the last time I saw him.' She peered across the crowded waiting area then turned to him and smiled sweetly. 'Anyway, I won't keep you. What I have to say can wait until you aren't so busy.'

She walked away, leaving Ben feeling like a complete idiot. Holly knew he'd been lying and all it had done was to make her even more suspicious. He made his way to the staffroom, wondering what he was going to do. He couldn't keep making excuses to avoid her but how could he be sure that he wouldn't cave in and tell her the truth? Part of him— a rather large part, too—wanted to tell her the whole story from start to finish, but the other bit knew how risky it would be. He couldn't afford to let Holly become so overwhelmed by pity that she suggested they try again because he mightn't have the strength to refuse.

The first hour was unusually slow so Ben filled in the time by catching up with some paperwork rather than spending it brooding. He'd just finished filling in the previous week's statistics sheet when Sean came into the office with the new paramedic.

'Ben, I'd like you to meet Gabriel McAndrew. He's been working with the Shropshire ambulance service for the past year but he's decided to make the move north and has joined our team as of today.'

'Nice to meet you,' Ben said, standing up to shake hands with the newcomer. He frowned as he looked at the other man. 'Have we met somewhere before? Your face looks really familiar.'

'We may have done.' Gabriel shrugged. 'I worked in London for a while so we could have run into each other there. Sean told me that you'd come here from St Gertrude's.'

'That's right,' Ben agreed, pleased to have solved the mystery. 'I expect I saw you when I was working in the A and E department there. It was so busy that you never got the chance to find out people's names.'

'I see you've been sorting out last week's stats.'

Sean claimed his attention at that moment and Ben turned to him. 'I thought I'd get them done while it was slack for once. You don't mind, I hope?'

'Definitely not! It's saved me a job.' Sean picked up the sheet and glanced at the figures. 'The rapid response team attended fifteen call-outs? That's not bad for our first week in operation, is it?'

'It isn't. And when you look at our success rate in saving lives then I think it proves the new service is having a positive effect,' Ben said, pointing to the last column.

'It certainly does.' Sean beamed as he handed back the sheet of paper. 'This calls for a celebration. Spread the word that everyone is invited to a barbecue at my house on Saturday night, will you, Ben? We deserve a bit of fun after all the hard work we've put in!'

'Will do.'

Ben sighed as he sat back down at the desk after the two men had left because he really didn't want to go to the barbecue. It wasn't that he was against socialising with the people he worked with but it would mean him socialising with Holly. He was ninety-nine per cent certain that he could behave sensibly if he kept her at a distance but he couldn't put such a high figure on it if they spent time together. It looked as though another excuse might be needed for Saturday night.

The week flew past so that Saturday arrived almost before Holly had time to draw breath. Everyone was in high spirits at the thought of the coming party when she went into work that morning. There was much talk in the staffroom about what they were all wearing and who they were going with.

Holly managed to be vague when Mandy asked if she was going with Josh by muttering something about not having seen him all week. It was true but only because she'd deliberately avoided him. Even though they'd made tentative arrangements to go out again, it hadn't seemed fair to encourage him when everything was still so uncertain between her and Ben. Of course, once she resolved that issue then maybe she would be in a better position to know what she was going to do but so far she'd not had a chance to sort things out.

If she'd been avoiding Josh, then Ben had definitely been avoiding her. She'd not said more than a dozen words to him since she'd met him in the foyer on Monday and those had all been work-related. Whenever she came into the department, he always seemed to be on his way out, and when they'd been asked to respond to a couple of serious incidents, Ben had managed to team up with one of the others. However, as Holly draped her stethoscope around her neck, she promised herself that she wouldn't let him escape that night.

The day was the usual blend of high drama and the mundane. The struggle to save a toddler who'd fallen into a garden pond was played out at the same time as a man was being treated for a splinter in his hand. Holly dealt with the child, using the motorbike because there was a football match on in town and everywhere was gridlocked with traffic. Fortunately, the toddler's grandfather had managed to resuscitate him by the time she got to the house but Holly's main fear was that the water the child had ingested might have washed all the pulmonary surfactant from his lungs. Pulmonary surfactant was as vital to the lungs as oil was to an engine—it prevented the lungs collapsing after a person breathed out. That led to hypoxia—an insufficient supply of oxygen reaching the tissues—and could prove fatal.

She quickly inserted an endotracheal airway, thanking her lucky stars that the muscles in the child's throat had relaxed enough for her to slide the tube into place. Oxygen came next and she carefully adjusted the flow so she didn't damage the little boy's lungs by using too high a pressure.

'He will be all right? I mean, he's breathing again so he's going to be fine, isn't he?'

'Let's hope so.' Holly looked up from stripping off the child's wet clothing when the grandfather spoke. The poor man was obviously dreadfully shocked by what had happened. 'I'll call an ambulance to take him to the hospital in a moment.'

'Oh, is that really necessary? My son will go mad when he hears what's happened. He warned me to cover up the pond when he brought Jack round this morning.' The old man suddenly sank onto the couch. 'My son is divorced, you see, so I don't get to see Jack all that often.'

Holly frowned in concern as she covered little Jack with a blanket because his grandfather looked really awful now. 'Are you all right? You don't look so good.'

'I'm fine. Don't worry about me, Doctor. You just concentrate on the youngster.'

He lay back against the cushions and closed his eyes. Holly grimaced when she heard how laboured his breathing sounded because it looked as though she might have another patient on her hands. She checked the little boy again and felt her heart lurch when she realised that his pulse rate was dropping. One of the side effects of a near drowning was that some of the water that was swallowed was absorbed into the body and caused a volume overload. That could lead to circulatory problems and little Jack was starting to exhibit all the signs.

She hunted her radio out of her pocket and called base, keeping a close eye on the child as she explained that she urgently needed back-up. She'd just finished when the little boy arrested. At the same moment his grandfather gasped and slumped sideways on the couch.

'Great!' Holly muttered, grabbing the defibrillator. 'Just what I needed. Two for the price of one!'

She quickly adjusted the dials then tossed back the blanket and applied the paddles to Jack's chest. Fortunately, the defib worked its magic so she covered the little boy up again and made sure his airway was clear and that he was still getting oxygen before she went to check on his grandfather. The old man was unconscious but he was still breathing and his heart was beating, thankfully enough.

'Hello! Anyone home?'

She looked round in relief when she heard Ben's voice calling through the letterbox. 'We're in the back…use the side gate, will you? I can't come to the door right now,' she shouted, hoping he would hear her.

He appeared a few seconds later, taking in the scene at a glance as he came into the room through the French windows. 'I'll look after the man if you want to concentrate on the child, Holly. Get onto base and explain that we have two patients, will you, Gabriel?' he directed, turning to the paramedic who had followed him in. 'They'll need to alert the rest of the team so they know what to expect.'

Holly gladly relinquished her place by the couch and went to kneel beside the child again. His pulse was still far too slow for her liking. He was obviously in shock and she came to a swift decision.

'He needs to be in hospital and I don't think it's safe to wait while you sort out his grandfather.'

'Then you and Gabriel take him back in the ambulance. I'll stay here and wait for another ambulance to arrive.' Ben checked the old man's pulse. 'He's holding his own and it's far more urgent that you get the child sorted out.'

'That would be great,' Holly agreed gratefully. Gabriel came back so she quickly explained what was happening, relieved when the paramedic didn't question the decision but merely picked up the oxygen bottle while she carried the child. They headed for the door where Holly paused for a moment. 'What about the motorbike and all my equipment?'

'I'll pack it up when the paramedics get here and ride the bike back.'

'Thanks. I owe you one for this, Ben. You're a lifesaver—in more ways than one!'

'All part of the service,' he said lightly, but she saw the warmth that had lit his face before he turned away and felt an answering glow start to burn inside her.

As she carried the little boy to the ambulance, Holly found herself thinking how easy it had been to restore harmony. All it had taken had been a few pleasant words and they'd been back to where they'd been two years ago—sharing a moment of closeness, their thoughts in sync, their problems forgotten…

She sighed as she laid little Jack on the trolley. If only it were that simple!

Malcolm Meadows had suffered a TIA—a transient ischaemic attack, more commonly known as a mini-stroke—undoubtedly brought on by the shock of seeing his grandson nearly drown. By the time the second ambulance arrived, Ben was fairly confident about his diagnosis, although it would need a CT scan to confirm it.

'You're going to be fine so try not to worry.' He squeezed the old man's shoulder, knowing how scary it must be for him to suddenly find himself so helpless. The brief interruption to the blood supply to Malcolm's brain had left him unable to speak or use his right arm and leg. However, Ben was hoping he would make a full recovery—like most people did—in a few days' time.

He went back inside the house after the ambulance drove away. Holly had left the defibrillator on the sitting-room floor so he packed it away then zipped up the Thomas pack and carried it outside. She'd left her helmet outside the French doors so Ben picked it up because he would need to wear it for the journey back to the hospital.

He put it on and was adjusting the chin strap when he became aware of a familiar fragrance. He breathed deeply and felt his heart lurch when he realised it was the scent of the shampoo Holly used. The fragrance must have permeated the lining of the helmet and it was like being enveloped in a great sea of memories as he drank it in. Being with Holly had been the high point of his life. Every day had been more wonderful, more special, because she'd shared it with him. They'd been too busy with work and too broke to do more than have the odd night out but it hadn't mattered. They hadn't needed expensive meals or exotic holidays because they'd had each other.

Had he been a fool to give her up? Should he have told her the truth about his illness and left it up to her to decide what she'd wanted to do?

He'd never asked himself those questions before and it was a salutary experience to find himself beset by doubts all of a sudden. He'd done what he'd thought right at the time but had it been his decision to make? Shouldn't he at least have given her the option to choose if she wanted to stay with him?

Ben swung his leg over the motorbike and kicked the engine to life, his heart beating in time to the rhythm of the powerful engine as another question slammed into his head: was he just looking for an *excuse* to tell her the truth because he couldn't bear the thought of living the rest of his life without her?

Sean had told everyone that it was open house and that they should turn up whenever they liked for the barbecue that evening. With staff working twenty-four/seven it was always difficult to arrange an event like this so timing had to be flexible. Holly was glad that she didn't need to be there at a set time because it was really late when she got home.

Little Jack Meadows had been transferred to Paediatric ICU and was currently on a ventilator. He would need treatment to correct an electrolyte imbalance caused by excess water being absorbed into his vascular system. He was a very sick little boy but Holly was hopeful that he would pull through.

His grandfather had been admitted to the coronary care unit. Apparently, he suffered from angina and that, combined with the TIA, meant he would need to be closely monitored for the next twenty-four hours. Holly had had the dubious of honour of explaining what had happened to Steven Meadows, Malcolm's son and Jack's father, when he'd arrived at the hospital. It had been a lot for the poor man to take in and that was what had delayed her.

She took a hasty shower then dressed in cream linen trousers and a honey-coloured silk top. The outfit was casual but elegant and seemed to fit the occasion, plus she really didn't have the time to agonise over what she was going to wear. A touch of lip gloss, several coats of mascara and she was ready. As she picked up her bag, Holly refused to acknowledge that the sudden fluttering in her stomach had anything to do with nerves. She was going to make Ben tell her the truth that night and there was no reason why she should feel nervous about it. After all, he couldn't tell her anything that would make her feel worse than she'd done when he'd ended their relationship.

The party was in full swing by the time she arrived and there was quite a crowd gathered in the garden. Everywhere looked very festive with rows of col-oured fairy lights strung up between the trees and old-fashioned Japanese lanterns hanging from hooks to light the patio. Sean was hard at work behind the barbecue and he waved to her.

'Glad you made it. Grab yourself a drink then come and give your order to the chef!'

'Will do!' Holly grinned as she followed a hand-written sign informing her that drinks were being served in the kitchen. From the look of the rather wobbly letters, one of the children must have made it. Sean's wife, Claire, was dispensing drinks from the kitchen table and she smiled in delight when she saw Holly.

'Oh, how lovely to see you!'

'You, too.' Holly gave her a hug then smiled at the little boy standing beside her. 'Hi, Ben. Am I right to think that brilliant sign out there was all your doing?'

'Did you see it?' the boy asked eagerly. 'I told Dad that we needed a sign and he asked me to make it for him.'

'It was a great idea,' Holly said seriously. 'I wouldn't have known where to go if I hadn't seen it.'

The child beamed with pleasure as he raced off to join his friends. Claire chuckled as she took a clean wineglass out of the box on the table. 'You just made his day. There's nothing Ben loves more than being in the thick of things. He obviously takes after his father!'

'He does, and in more ways than one. He's the absolute image of Sean, apart from his hair colour, of course—he's more like you in that respect.'

'I know. It's amazing, isn't it? His sister, Amy, has Sean's black hair and my colour eyes—just as if everything has been reversed.' Claire sounded dreamy. 'I wonder what the next one will look like.'

'Does that mean what I think it does?' Holly exclaimed, then laughed in delight when Claire nodded. 'Congratulations! So when is the new baby due?'

'Eight months from now.' Claire blushed. 'I only found out this morning and we were planning on keeping it a secret but I'm going to burst if I don't tell someone soon!'

'I think it's wonderful and I'm really happy for you,' Holly said sincerely then glanced round when someone came into the kitchen.

Her blood suddenly began to fizz when she saw it was Ben—the adult Ben and not the child this time. She bit her lip as a dozen different emotions hit her all at once, ranging from appreciation because he looked so handsome in those black chinos and matching polo shirt right the way up to pure terror because of what she was planning on doing. All of

a sudden she was no longer sure if she was doing
the right thing. Did she really want to risk getting
hurt all over again just to learn the answers to a few
questions?

'Hi! Sorry I'm so late.'

Ben had been one hundred per cent certain that he
wasn't going to attend the barbecue that night. He'd
even told Sean that he wouldn't be there, claiming
that he had a prior engagement. He'd gone into work
that day secure in the knowledge that he wasn't going to put himself to the test by attending the party,
so what had made him change his mind? The fact
that he was suddenly having doubts about the decisions he'd made two years ago?

'So long as you got here, it doesn't matter about
the time,' Claire assured him. 'What will you have
to drink?'

'Do you have any beer?' He summoned a smile
but it was hard to appear calm. Not only did he have
to contend with his own ambivalence but Holly was
staring at him as though he'd suddenly sprouted a
second head. He had no idea what was wrong with
her but it definitely didn't bode well for the evening.

'We most certainly do,' Claire replied cheerfully,
opening the fridge. She groaned. 'Drat! It's all gone.
Hang on a sec and I'll fetch some more from the
garage.'

She hurried away before Ben could tell her it
didn't matter and he grimaced. 'I didn't mean to send
her rushing about after me.'

'I'm sure she doesn't mind,' Holly replied dis-

tantly. She picked up her glass and sidled towards
the door and, perversely, Ben realised that he didn't
want her to leave. So maybe he'd been mad to come,
and crazier still to think about raking up the past, but
putting all that aside there was no reason why they
couldn't spend a few minutes together, was there?

'I saw you talking to Steven Meadows when he
arrived at the hospital,' he said, hurriedly latching
onto a relatively safe topic. 'It must have been a
shock when he found out that both his son and his
father were in hospital.'

'It was.' Holly took a sip of her wine then ran her
finger over the condensation that had formed on the
outside of the glass.

Ben's stomach muscles spasmed as he found himself imagining just how cool her fingertip would feel
if it touched his skin. Goose-bumps suddenly sprang
up all over his body and he had to breathe in and
out a couple of times before he could concentrate on
what she was saying—something about the Meadows
family, if he wasn't mistaken.

'I checked on little Jack before I left tonight,' he
said rather thickly when she paused. 'There's been
no change but at least his condition hasn't deterio-
rated.'

'That's something to be grateful for.'

She edged a little closer to the door and Ben
rushed on, wondering what on earth was the matter
with him. Why didn't he let her leave and just thank
his lucky stars that she wasn't going to say anything
that would make his life even more difficult?

'The grandfather is doing fine as well. He's got

some movement back in his right side and his speech is coming back, although he's still having problems finding the odd word at times.'

'Good. I'm glad to hear it,' she said mildly, taking another step.

'And I signed in the motorbike and all the equipment as well.' He shrugged when she glanced at him. 'Everything is in order so you don't need to worry about it.'

'I'm not.'

She took another step then stopped. Ben could almost *feel* her indecision as she stood stock still for a moment. When she turned towards him, he couldn't decide if he was glad or sorry that he'd detained her, especially when he saw her chin lift. Holly was preparing herself for what might lie ahead and her bravery filled him with pride and sadness in roughly equal measures. She was just as unsure about what she was doing as he was but she wasn't going to let it stop her. She was the most wonderful woman he'd ever known and it didn't make him feel good to realise that he might end up hurting her again.

'What's going on, Ben? You've been avoiding me all week so why do I get the feeling that you suddenly want to talk to me? Has something else happened?'

'Something else?' he repeated, playing for time because he still wasn't sure if he was going to carry this through to the possibly bitter end. 'I didn't know anything had happened in the first place.'

She clicked her tongue in response to his pedantry. 'You know very well what I mean so let's not split hairs. You knew I wanted to talk to you which is why you've kept out of my way, but all of a sudden *you're* the one who wants to talk and it doesn't make sense. What is this all about? If it has anything to do with what happened two years ago, I think I have a right to know.'

CHAPTER TEN

'Look, Holly—'

'Sorry about the wait.'

Claire came back with the beer and Ben stopped.
Out of the corner of his eye he saw Holly leaving
but there was nothing he could do about it. He
thanked Claire for the drink then hurried outside but
Holly had already gone to join the other guests. He
watched her greeting Mandy and Kwame and turned
away because there was no point trying to speak to
her now. If—and it was a very big *if* at this stage—
he did decide to tell her the truth, he needed to talk
to her on her own.

He got himself a burger from the barbecue then
sat down on a bench under the apple tree because he
needed a few minutes alone to get his head round
this problem. A few more people arrived and he
waved when he spotted Nicky and Gabriel amongst
them. He knew that Josh was working that night because he'd checked the rosters, but in a perverse way
he wished the other man had been there. It might
have stopped *him* doing something foolish if Josh
had been around. After all, what good would come
of telling Holly the truth? What would it achieve?
All it would do was to confuse the issue.

His mind raced but he still hadn't decided what he
was going to do when someone switched on the

stereo. As Ben watched, Sean handed the barbecue tongs to Kwame then led Claire onto the patio and took her in his arms. They looked so blissfully unaware of everyone else as they swayed in time to the music that it brought a lump to Ben's throat. He knew how they felt because he'd felt that way too once upon a time. He'd only needed to hold Holly and the world and its problems had disappeared like magic. How he longed to recapture that feeling but it was too much to hope he could ever feel that way again. He and Holly were two very different people now and they could never go back to the way they'd been.

His heart felt like lead as he stood up. He'd been wrong to come here tonight and the best thing he could do now was to leave before he made a mess of everything. He headed across the garden, hoping he could slip away without anyone noticing, but just at that moment Nicky came hurrying over and grabbed hold of his hand.

'My dance, I think, Dr Carlisle. Come along!'

Ben could hardly refuse and had no choice other than to follow her onto the patio. Fortunately, the music had changed to a tune that everyone knew so there were a lot of people dancing now. He saw Kwame dancing with Mandy then spotted Alison and her husband and smiled at them. Nicky gyrated around him, wiggling her hips and receiving a spontaneous roar of encouragement from the crowd. Ben tried to look as though he was having fun but he'd just spotted Holly dancing with Max and it was hard to focus on anything else…

He frowned because the surgeon was holding Holly far too close to his way of thinking. This was a fast number so why did Max need to hang onto her like that? By the time the track ended, Ben could feel his hackles rising and knew he had to make his escape, only Nicky had started dancing again and he couldn't just walk off and leave her. He gritted his teeth and turned so that he wouldn't have to see what Holly was doing.

Max had definitely had too much to drink, Holly decided as she removed his hand from her bottom and placed it firmly back on her waist. As soon as the music stopped she would make her escape, probably call it a night and go home. There was no point staying because she'd realised how stupid it would be to try and talk to Ben. It wouldn't achieve anything—it would just create more problems. It would be far better to leave things the way they were.

She and Max negotiated another uncoordinated turn and she suddenly found herself facing Ben. She blinked because she had no idea what she'd done to warrant the glare he gave her. Another turn and they'd danced past him but Max's hand was starting to wander again and she suddenly decided that, good manners or not, she'd had enough.

'Sorry, Max, it's time I left.' She steered him towards a seat, shaking her head when he tried to grab her hand. 'No. You're going to feel very embarrassed in the morning so let's not make matters any worse.'

She left him there, rolling her eyes when Mandy gave her a sympathetic smile as she passed. Sean and

Claire were still locked in each other's arms and Holly didn't want to disturb them so she decided to slip away without saying her goodbyes. She could always phone tomorrow and thank them then.

She headed straight for the gate and had almost reached it when someone came hurrying round the side of the house. Her heart leapt into her throat when she realised it was Ben because she didn't want to have to speak to him now that she'd made up her mind to leave things the way they were.

'I was just going home,' she said, quickly unlatching the gate. 'I'll see you at work.' She went to close the gate behind her then stopped when she discovered Ben had followed her out.

'I'm heading home as well.' He shut the gate with a sharp little click then smiled rather grimly at her. 'Do I take it that you've had enough of being mauled?'

'Max has had a bit too much to drink, that's all,' she replied coolly, wondering why she felt the need to defend Max when he'd been such a pest.

'And that's an excuse for his behaviour, is it?'

Holly blinked when she heard the rumble of anger in his voice. 'No, but it probably explains it. No doubt Max will be mortified when he remembers what happened in the morning.'

'Let's hope so. It might teach him to keep his hands to himself in future.'

His tone was sharp enough to draw blood and Holly stopped and stared at him. 'I'm sure Max will be suitably repentant but don't tell me you've never made a bit of a fool of yourself when you've had one too many.'

'I've never mauled a woman if that's what you mean. But maybe you didn't see it as that. Maybe you enjoyed the attention.'

Holly was so shocked that she could barely breathe, let alone speak. She just stared at him in utter amazement and saw a wash of colour run up his face.

'I'm sorry,' he bit out. 'I had no right to say that.'

'You had no right even to *think* it, let alone say it!' All of a sudden her voice came back and she rounded on him. 'Who the hell do you think you are, Ben? You don't own me and you certainly don't have the right to pass insulting comments like that!'

'I know, and I've said I'm sorry!' He ran his hand through his hair and she was shocked when she saw that he was trembling.

'Then make sure you don't say anything like it again,' she instructed, her anger sliding a notch or two down the scale from white hot to merely red.

'I won't. It's just…' He stopped and shook his head. 'It doesn't matter.'

'It's just—*what*?' She put her hand on his arm when he went to walk away and felt the frisson that immediately rippled under his skin. She snatched her hand away again because she couldn't deal with the thought that Ben still responded to her touch when this needed sorting out.

'What were you going to say before you thought better of it?' she prompted in what she hoped was a reasonable tone.

'It really doesn't matter, Holly…'

'Of course it does!'

'Why? What possible reason could you have for wanting to know what I think or how I feel?' He laughed harshly and the sound made her wince because it was so filled with pain.

'Because we used to love each other, Ben, and I still…care about you.'

'And I still care about you, Holly, which is why we should leave things the way they are.' He brushed her cheek with his knuckles in what was probably supposed to be nothing more than a friendly gesture of reassurance, but the response it generated was alarming.

From both of them.

Holly's breath caught in an audible gasp when she felt the gentle pressure of his fingers on her skin but Ben's gasp was even louder. She stared at him as they both stood there in the street as though rooted to the spot. There was no moon that night and his face was shadowy, lacking in colour, so that it was like looking at a negative rather than a real flesh-and-blood man. A man who had the power to give her life all the colour she could ever need. She loved him so much that all she needed was Ben and her life would be forever filled with rainbows and sunshine.

She wasn't aware of moving but she must have done because all of a sudden they were standing toe to toe and she was staring into his eyes with all the love she'd tried to deny these two long years clear to see. She saw his pupils dilate with shock and touched him—just lightly—on the chest because she needed the contact every bit as much as she needed air and food and warmth and shelter to exist. Her fingers splayed across his breastbone and stayed there while she felt his heart pounding beneath her palm.

'Holly, we mustn't…we shouldn't…we…'

Her lips fitted so perfectly to his that the rest of the sentence was sealed inside his mouth. All she was left with was the warm rush of air as the words tried to get out but it was enough because she understood what he was trying to tell her. *This is silly. It could create more problems. And look what had happened the last time we kissed each other—we ended up in bed together!*

Her mouth tilted at the corners because it was all true but she wasn't going to let *that* stop her. She was going to kiss Ben because it was what they both needed to survive!

She stood on tiptoe, leaning against him for support as she seduced him with her mouth. His lips were so stubborn at first—staying tightly shut and refusing to soften—but she wasn't deterred. Her own lips parted as she allowed the tip of her tongue to trace the outline of his and she felt his heart leap beneath her palm. Good. A *positive* response at last.

Her tongue performed another circuit, pausing *en route* to enjoy the chiselled perfection of his Cupid's bow and the deliciously sexy fullness of his bottom lip. She wasn't an expert on mouths, by any means, but Ben's had to be in the top one per cent of irresistible lips. It definitely came top of her own personal list.

'This is crazy.' He dragged his mouth away and glared at her. 'Holly, do you realise how bloody stupid it is to stand here kissing me?'

'Mmm, I suppose it is rather public,' she replied dreamily. 'Let's go somewhere a bit more private, shall we?'

'No!' He grabbed hold of her hand and pushed her away. 'We've been down that road before, remember, and it didn't help.'

'Because we went down it for the wrong reason,' she said simply. 'I thought I could get you out of my system by sleeping with you one last time but all it did was make me feel more mixed up about what I wanted.'

'Then that just proves it would be madness to do it a second time, doesn't it?'

'No. What it proves, Ben, is that I'm still not over you. I can't be if I feel this way. Oh, I've tried, believe me, because I didn't want to admit that I still loved you—but I do.' She looked him straight in the eyes, praying they would be able to find a way round whatever problems they had to face.

'I asked Josh out purely and simply because I wanted to prove to myself that that I didn't need you any more.' She shrugged. 'It didn't work. That's all I can say. I know we have problems to sort out and I suspect they stem from something that happened two years ago. But unless we get everything out into the open, I don't think either of us will ever be able to get on with our lives.'

She laughed mirthlessly, feeling the prickle of tears stinging her lids because it was still so painful to recall what had happened. 'I'd hate to imagine myself being old and grey and still not know the real reason why you dumped me.'

'And I'd love to be able to picture myself as being old and grey,' he said flatly and with so little emotion that her heart seemed to stall.

'What do you mean by that?' she whispered.

'That there is no guarantee I'll live long enough to be old or grey.' He took her hands and gripped them so hard that she winced but he didn't appear to notice. 'In fact, if I had to lay odds on it happening then I'd have to put them very low indeed. I had cancer, Holly, and the truth is that I have no idea how long I might live.'

Ben had thought about this moment many times and more so in the last few weeks. He'd pictured himself telling Holly about his illness and each time the scene had been set so perfectly. Maybe it would happen in a restaurant over a delicious meal when they were both feeling relaxed, or down by the river because that had become an increasingly attractive option since he'd moved to Dalverston. There was something about being close to water that was soothing and that would help to ease the shock. The one place he'd never imagined himself breaking the news to her had been in the middle of a street and he realised what a terrible mistake he'd made when he felt her sway.

'Here. Lean on me.' He put his arm around her

waist and somehow managed to get her back through the gate then couldn't decide where to go. He couldn't take her back to the party in this state yet he couldn't just keep her standing there either. He was in a quandary when Claire suddenly appeared and he heard her gasp of dismay when she saw them.

'Holly's feeling a bit faint,' he explained quickly. 'Would you mind if I took her inside?'

'Of course not!' Claire led the way, opening the door to the sitting-room. 'Can I get her a drink of water or maybe coffee would be best?'

'No, thanks.' Ben grimaced because he'd hate Claire to think that Holly was drunk. 'She's had a bit of a shock, I'm afraid. She just needs to sit quietly for a few minutes.'

'Oh, I see. In that case, I'll leave you two alone.'

Claire hurriedly retreated, closing the door behind her as she went. Ben sat Holly down on the sofa then pulled over a footstool and sat down in front of her. Taking hold of her cold hands, he gently chafed them. 'I am so sorry, sweetheart. I should never have sprung it on you like that.'

'How did you intend to tell me, then? Over a glass of wine at the pub? Or maybe in between seeing patients? You could have slipped it in while we were out on a call, couldn't you? *Oh, by the way, Holly, I forgot to tell you that I had cancer and could die but let's not worry about it while we're busy.*'

She laughed harshly and Ben winced because it was a little too near to the truth. 'I'm sorry. And, yes, you're right because if I had got round to telling you then I'd probably have chosen a time like that.'

'If? Obviously, you hadn't made up your mind about it. Is that why you've been so evasive of late? Because you weren't sure if I deserved to know the truth at last?'

'It wasn't a question of you *deserving* to know. I was trying to…well, weigh up the damage it might cause.'

'Damage to whom?' she snapped with a pedantry which put him instantly on his guard.

'To you, of course. The whole reason I didn't tell you in the first place was because I wanted to spare you any distress.' He let go of her hands because he couldn't continue to touch her and think rationally. 'It didn't seem right to wreck your life as well as mine.'

'And who appointed you as my guardian angel?'

'I'm sorry…?'

'It's quite simple, Ben. I really don't know why you have a problem understanding an easy question like that, but let me phrase it in a different way. Who put you in charge of my life? Who said that you could make my decisions? I certainly don't remember giving you that kind of authority.'

'It wasn't like that!'

He got up and strode to the window then came all the way back, his footsteps thumping on the wooden floor. 'I suddenly found out that I had cancer of the colon and that I needed treatment. Oh, the consultant tried to put a positive spin on the prognosis but you know as well as I do that there are no guarantees. It knocked me for six and all I could think about was how wrong it would be if you suffered because I was ill.'

'So you told me that you'd met someone else and no longer loved me? Nice, Ben, very nice. It must have taken a lot of imagination to come up with a story like that.'

'I just didn't want you thinking that you *had* to stay with me! You had your career to think about, all the plans you'd made for the future…'

'Don't you mean all the plans *we'd* made?' She laughed and he winced when he heard the pain in her voice. 'My life was so tied up with yours that they were *our* dreams, *our* hopes and *our* ambitions. Or that's what I naïvely believed. I thought we could conquer the world together but when it came down to it, *you* made *your* decision and didn't consult me.'

'I did it because I loved you! Because I cared and wanted what was best for you!' He stood in front of her, willing her to believe him because this was worse than he'd ever imagined it would be. 'There were so many things to take in—not just if the treatment would work and how long I might live, but the fact that I could be sterile afterwards.'

'And are you?' she asked with a catch in her voice. 'I don't know.'

He sat down abruptly on the stool and took hold of her hands again because suddenly he needed something to cling to. 'I've never had the inclination to find out. It just didn't seem to matter if I could father a child after we split up because I only ever wanted you to have my children, Holly. Nobody else.'

Suddenly he was crying and he bowed his head in shame at his own weakness. He needed to be strong for Holly's sake but he'd spent two long years living with his broken dreams and he had no reserves left. Holly murmured something and then her arms were around him, holding him while he sobbed, sobbing with him so that her tears fell into his hair. It seemed an age before he found the strength to raise his head but it might have been only minutes for all he knew. The length of time didn't matter, only that he'd finally told her the truth. Now he had to be very careful what he did in case he ruined things again. He'd wanted to protect Holly two years ago and even though he might have been wrong to go about it the way he had, the desire was just as strong now as it had ever been. He would lay down his life without another thought if it would keep her safe.

'I'm sorry, Holly. Can you forgive me?'

'I suppose I'll have to because we certainly can't stay in here crying our eyes out much longer.'

'Mmm, you're right.' He smiled at her, loving her all the more for trying to make him feel better. 'Sean and Claire could get a little miffed if we take over their sitting-room permanently.'

He brushed the tears off her cheeks then kissed her gently on the mouth, just a single kiss because it was all he could allow himself even though he wanted dozens more. Holly had been deeply moved by his story but he didn't want her making any hasty decisions out of pity.

His stomach churned because the thought of becoming an object of pity in her eyes was more than he could bear. He simply wouldn't risk it! Couldn't and wouldn't accept the crumbs of her love when he'd once had the whole. Their love had been as bright as the sun, as deep as the ocean and as vast as the heavens, and he would never, *ever* settle for anything less.

'So, now that we've finally sorted everything out, what are we going to do, Ben?'

He stood up, picking up the footstool and putting it carefully back in its rightful place. 'There isn't much we can do. I'm sorry for the lies I told you, Holly. Really, really sorry.'

'I know that,' she said quickly and with a touch of impatience that made his nerves knot. 'I'm not talking about what happened two years ago but about what's going to happen from here on. What you just told me changes everything—'

'No, it doesn't.' He turned to face her and smiled, even though his heart felt as though it was caving in on itself. 'It doesn't change a thing, Holly. It can't do because I won't let it.'

'Meaning that you don't want us to try again?'

'It wouldn't be right.'

He tried to blot out the shock in her voice because he couldn't let himself dwell on it. If he gave himself any leeway he would simply agree with whatever she suggested and it wouldn't be right for them to live that way—her loving him out of pity, him hating himself for not being the man she deserved.

'Fifty per cent of people who are treated for bowel cancer live for five years or more. Those are the statistics but they aren't a guarantee. I've had two of those five years and I have no idea if I'll have the other three or not. The cancer could come back this year, next year—'

'Or ten, even twenty years from now. And it might never come back at all!' she countered fiercely. 'Don't quote statistics at me, Ben, because I'll quote them right back at you! If there is no guarantee that you are going to live then, equally, there's no guarantee that you are going to die either!'

'I know that, darling.' He grimaced as the endearment slipped out because it would be wrong to let her think he was softening. 'We could stand here until the moon turns blue and argue the point but the truth is it makes no difference. I won't change my mind because there are too many factors stacked up in the minus column that sum up my future. You deserve more than I can give you, Holly, and that's it.'

'And it's not open to negotiation? You've made all the decisions again just like you did before?'

'Yes. Call me a dyed-in-the-wool chauvinist but I won't ruin your life just because my own is in doubt.' He took a deep breath but the words had to be said because he owed her the truth. Every bit of it.

'I love you, Holly. I love you too much to let you waste yourself on me.'

CHAPTER ELEVEN

I LOVE you, Holly. I love you too much to let you waste yourself on me.

The words haunted Holly in the following weeks. She knew that Ben had wanted to be completely honest with her but several times she found herself wishing that he hadn't told her how he really felt. She loved him too, and had told him so, but words simply weren't enough. They couldn't erase the horror of his illness or the fear of it returning. They couldn't prove or disprove that he was right to take this stance. They couldn't convince him that she was prepared to face any hardship if it meant they could be together. Words couldn't make him see that she loved him despite of his illness and loved him because of it, and she didn't know what to do or where to turn.

In an effort to stave off the misery of knowing how little chance she had of making Ben see sense, Holly threw herself into her work, arriving early and staying long after she was due to go home. A few people commented on her dedication but nobody questioned her, not even Nicky, thankfully. Nicky had been seeing rather a lot of Gabriel since the night of the barbecue so Holly spent many evenings on her own in the flat. It was time she came to dread because she spent it thinking about Ben and his illness and what it might mean. It was as though her head was filled with him and she couldn't shut him out even if she wanted to, which she didn't. She wanted to love him and care for him in sickness and in health—please, God, it would be the latter and not the former—but he was too stubborn to accept that. It was no wonder that she was glad when it was time to go to work because it meant she had to think about something else.

Three weeks after the barbecue and Ben's bombshell the rapid response team found themselves facing their biggest challenge. Sean looked grim as he called everyone into the office and explained that there'd been an explosion at a laboratory in the new business park. The number of casualties was as yet unknown but there had been two hundred staff working there when it had happened and only a fraction of them had been accounted for so far. It was a major incident so they would be deploying all their resources—helicopter, four-wheel-drive, motorbike and ambulances. Off-duty staff had been recalled and even before Sean finished speaking the first of them began arriving. Ben was amongst them and Holly tried to curb the lurch her heart gave when Sean told them they would be working as part of the helicopter team.

Ben held the door for her as they left the office. The whole department was buzzing and Holly could feel the tension in the air as she ran to the storeroom and wriggled into a flight-suit. Helmet, boots, Thomas pack, torch—she mentally ticked off the list because at least it meant she didn't have to think about Ben, who was also getting ready. It would be the first time they'd worked together since the barbecue because they'd been on opposite shifts since then, but she mustn't let it affect her performance.

'Ready?'

Ben's tone was clipped and her heart jerked like a puppet on a string because she could tell he was equally nervous. 'Yes,' she replied just as shortly and no more sweetly as she hurried out of the room.

The helicopter was on the pad with its engine running so she ducked low to avoid the downdraught from the rotors and scrambled on board. Ben swung himself inside then gave the mechanic the thumbs up to tell him to close the doors while Holly strapped herself in and picked up the headset which would allow her to communicate with the pilot. It was all so familiar now that she was able to go through the routine without a hitch and her confidence came flooding back. She wasn't going to fluff her lines because of Ben.

It took them just five minutes to reach the business park, which was clearly distinguishable by the pall of black smoke hanging over the area. Holly heard the pilot mutter something uncomplimentary as he struggled to find a suitable landing site because of the poor visibility. Touchdown was a little jerky but she didn't complain. She was just glad they'd landed in one piece.

Ben had the door unlocked before she'd even undone her safety harness and he jumped out and headed straight for the officer in charge without waiting for her. Holly followed as fast as she could although the bulky Thomas pack slowed her down somewhat. There were police and firemen all around and she could hear sirens wailing in the distance as more of the emergency services responded. She and Ben were the first medics on scene and she felt butterflies fluttering wildly in her stomach at the thought of what they might have to deal with.

'They've got just over a hundred people out so far, which means there's another hundred still inside the building.' Ben looked grim as he came back to update her. 'The main lab is the worst area, apparently. That's where the explosion occurred.'

'Was it chemicals?' Holly asked, because if it was then they might need protective suits. They were stored in the hold of the helicopter so at least they were to hand.

'A bomb. Apparently, there was a phone call to the local newspaper and that's why the police and fire brigade got here so quickly. They were on their way when the bomb went off.'

'A bomb!' Holly exclaimed in horror.

'Yep. Some guy with a grudge against the company. An ex-employee, apparently. The police have him in custody so at least we won't have to contend with some lunatic, running around inside the building. They're trying to find someone who can tell us what was being used in the lab. Looks like this might be him now.'

Holly turned as a police officer came hurrying over, accompanied by a tall man with greying hair who introduced himself as Simon Humphreys, the head of research.

'Can you tell us what you were working on?' Ben demanded.

'A new form of CS gas.' Simon Humphreys pushed a wispy strand of hair out of his eyes with a trembling hand. 'We've been perfecting a formula that causes less side-effects.'

'So does that mean there's none of the usual problems you'd expect from coming into contact with CS gas,' Holly queried hopefully. 'No stinging eyes, breathlessness or similar problems?'

'Yes and no. The effects are similar but not as intense so there's less of a risk to anyone breathing it in. However, today we were doing a controlled experiment to compare the CS gas used by the police with our new product.'

'So what you're saying is that both gases were in the lab when the explosion occurred?' Ben exclaimed in dismay.

'Yes. Obviously, the experiment was taking place in a sealed chamber but the problem is that I've no idea if it has been damaged.' Simon shook his head worriedly. 'I also can't say how the two gases might react with each other. That was one of our main concerns, in fact, and what we were going to establish next.'

'Then surely there's a serious risk to the public?' Holly stated, glancing pointedly at the cloud of smoke hanging over the whole area.

'Most of the gas will have dispersed before it can do any harm,' Simon assured her. 'However, the police are contacting the local schools and advising them to keep the children indoors, and the public is being told to keep their doors and windows shut. The real danger will be to anyone inside the lab. The concentration of gas will be much higher in there, plus there's a chance that the gas might revert to a powder form. That would cause severe skin irritation for anyone coming into contact with it.'

'Right, so we'll need to use the suits,' Ben said, turning to her. 'Can you get them while I let Control know what's happening? Anyone attending the incident will need protective clothing and we'll also need to set up a decontamination centre on site.'

'Sure.'

Holly ran back to the helicopter and with the pilot's help unpacked their equipment. She started to get ready, putting on an oxygen tank first then sliding the insulated, all-in-one garment over the top of her other clothing. The suit had a hood with a clear Perspex panel in the front to see through plus gloves and bootees to protect her hands and feet. She pulled the hood over her head and turned on the oxygen, checking the tank was functioning properly.

Ben started getting ready as well so within minutes they were on their way, the protective clothing feeling incredibly bulky and awkward as she walked. One of the fire crew, who was similarly attired, met them outside the building and explained that he would lead the way and that they were to follow his instructions and leave immediately if he decided they were in danger, so it was all very scary. Holly glanced at Ben and felt her heart lift when he winked at her. Maybe he was still determined to go it alone but she felt so much better knowing that he was with her.

The foyer of the building was relatively unscathed apart from all the shattered windows. The fire had been contained to the actual lab area and the closer they got, the hotter it became. It became increasingly difficult to see and Holly didn't hesitate when Ben offered her his hand. Even through the double thickness of their gloves she could feel his fingers gripping hers and it was a huge comfort. They reached the lab where the fireman quickly conferred in gestures with his colleagues who were dealing with the fire. He was obviously given the all-clear because a few seconds later he led them inside.

The first casualty was lying by the door and she was obviously dead. Holly quickly averted her eyes from the shattered body because it wasn't a pleasant sight. Two more people were lying under a workbench and they too were dead. Holly was just beginning to wonder if they would find anyone alive when Ben suddenly veered off to the side. She quickly turned and spotted a young man crouched beneath one of the huge industrial-sized sinks.

She hurriedly followed Ben, cursing the bulky clothing as she knelt down. The man was obviously in shock and didn't respond when Ben spoke to him. Holly could see that his left hand had been partly severed by flying glass and that he was having problems breathing, but he was alive and that was something.

She quickly fitted him with an oxygen mask while Ben attended to his hand. Once the bleeding was under control, they managed to rig up a sling out of some dressings. They got him to his feet and led him to the door, where the fire crew took over, then went back into the lab and found a young woman next with multiple injuries—stoved-in chest, broken arm, both legs, the list seemed endless. She was too badly injured to move without a stretcher so the fireman relayed their request and they made her comfortable with painkillers while they waited for it to arrive. Josh and Gabriel brought it in, suited up in protective clothing like theirs.

They got the poor woman onto the stretcher and sent her on her way then it was on to the next person and the next, each one seemingly more bloody and battered and shocked. By the time they left the lab over an hour later, Holly felt as though she'd just glimpsed what hell might be like.

A decontamination unit had been set up right outside the building so they were ushered straight there. They were hosed down then, in turn, stripped off their protective suits and went inside the unit where they had to undress completely and shower. Holly knew how vital it was to ensure that any chemical residue was thoroughly washed away so dutifully soaped and rinsed, although she would have felt much happier if the water had been hot instead of merely lukewarm. By the time she left the shower and slipped on a gown, her teeth were chattering and she gratefully accepted the cup of tea that was handed to her.

Ben followed her out a few minutes later, looking blue-tinged with cold and shivering so hard that his

teeth were chattering. Holly looked at him in concern. 'Are you OK? Here, have this tea. It will warm
you up.'

'No, you drink it. You need it just as much as I
do.'

He smiled but she'd seen the expression that had
flashed across his face and knew that he thought she
was worried because she was thinking about his cancer and everything. It was just so ridiculous that she
almost laughed out loud, only she knew that if she
started laughing then she'd end up crying. It made
her see how impossible it would be to live together
if every time she said something Ben would think
she was referring to his illness. Maybe it did loom
large in her thoughts—she didn't deny that—but Ben
was more to her than a body that had malfunctioned.
Ben was Ben and, with or without the cancer, she
would worry about him because that was all part of
loving someone—to care when they were ill and
want them to get better.

By the time the tea had been drunk, Holly was
feeling about as low as she could get and was glad
when the pilot came to tell them that they were returning to base. They landed at the hospital ten
minutes later and she immediately went to get
changed. She kept a spare set of clothes in her locker
so she took everything to the ladies' loo and got
dressed in there, using the hand-drier over the basins
to dry her wet hair, then went through to the department. The influx of patients from the explosion
meant that everyone who wasn't suffering from a
life-threatening injury had been asked to leave but

the place was still chock-full. Sean was in Resus, working on the young woman with the multiple injuries, and Max was in Theatre. The man with the partly severed hand had been sent upstairs and was currently being dealt with by the microsurgical team.

Holly filled in wherever she was needed, standing in for the nurses if it was necessary. She was part of the team and she wasn't averse to covering any gaps. She saw Ben briefly on his way to Men's Surgical with one of the firemen who'd been injured but there wasn't time to say anything to him. Anyway, what was there to say? *Yes, I care about you having cancer and worry if it will come back but it doesn't define you as a person. You are still the same person to me, the one I've always loved and always will.*

It was how she felt but putting feelings into words only seemed to dilute their meaning. Anyway, Ben should know how she felt without her having to tell him. He should know in his heart and his soul that nothing would change the way she thought of him, that to her he would always be the only man she would ever truly love.

The day seemed never-ending and Ben soon lost count of the number and range of injuries he dealt with. He did his job and did it well, but he'd tuned himself out. It was a defence mechanism because he'd seen sights that day he'd never expected to see outside a war zone. The thought that someone had deliberately inflicted such terrible injuries was too much to deal with so he tried to shut it all out and succeeded—to a point. However, each time he saw

Holly's pale, strained face his heart twisted that little bit more. He desperately wanted to comfort her but knew that he couldn't. He had to let her go for her sake if not for his own so it was a relief when she went home because at least he didn't have to continually fight his own instincts and emotions.

It was almost eight before he felt he could safely leave and he was so tired by then that he could hardly walk straight. He meandered towards the staffroom, groaning under his breath when Julie Kilbride, the night sister, called him over. He was tempted to ignore her but she had a man with her and Ben could tell they both wanted to speak to him.

'Ben, this is Jacqueline Baxter's husband…the lady from the laboratory with the M.I.' Julie waggled her eyebrows at him, obviously trying to convey some kind of message, but his brain was so clogged with tiredness and horror that it was hard to grasp what she meant.

'M.I,' he repeated uncertainly.

'Multiple injuries,' Julie mouthed behind the man's back, and the penny suddenly dropped.

Ben's heart sank because Jacqueline Baxter had been barely clinging to life when they'd sent her to ICU and he hadn't rated her chances very highly. 'I'm so sorry about your wife,' he said sincerely. 'I'm afraid I haven't had a chance to check how she is since we sent her upstairs to ICU.'

'Jackie died an hour ago.'

Ben grimaced. 'I'm very sorry.'

'Thank you.' Mr Baxter looked round and Julie nodded pointedly towards the relatives' room so Ben took the hint and shifted his exhausted brain up a gear.

'Perhaps you'd like to go somewhere a bit more private?'

'If you don't mind, Doctor. I mean, you were on your way home and I don't want to keep you...'

'It isn't a problem,' Ben assured him, and meant it. He led the way into the room and sat down, waiting patiently while Mr Baxter went to the window. The man was obviously trying to gather his thoughts and Ben didn't want to rush him.

'I just wanted to thank you for what you did, Dr Carlisle,' the man said at last, turning to him. 'One of the policemen told me that you and another doctor risked your lives by going into the lab and I want you to know how grateful I am.'

'I only wish we could have done more,' Ben said truthfully.

'So do I, but you can't perform miracles. Jackie was too badly hurt and I don't think anything could have saved her.' The man swallowed hard, struggling for control. 'At least I was able to be with her when she died and that's something I'll always be grateful for. Oh, she wasn't conscious but I know in here...' he tapped his chest '...that Jackie knew I was with her and that means so much to me. She's the only woman I've ever loved, you see. Just being with her made my life *mean* something. I hate it that we'll never be able to fulfil all our dreams but I had her for five precious years and nobody can take that away from me. Not ever!'

He broke off and started to sob. Ben wished with

all his heart that he could think of something to say that would help but he was afraid to speak in case he broke down himself and after a moment the man managed to collect himself.

'Anyway, that's all I wanted to say, Dr Carlisle, so I won't keep you any longer. Thank you for giving me that time with Jackie. I'm truly grateful to you.'

Ben stood up and shook his hand, murmuring something he hoped was appropriate although he had no idea what he'd said. Mr Baxter left after that but Ben sat down again because his legs would no longer support him. The man had been grateful for a few minutes and yet he was denying himself and Holly the chance of possibly having weeks, months or even *years* together. Why? Because he was afraid that she might pity him? Because he wanted more than crumbs? Because he was too bloody selfish to realise how lucky he was!

He stood up, his heart beating all out of sync so that he felt breathless and excited and scared at the same time. He was taking the coward's way out, running away because his emotions had been battered and bruised and he didn't want to risk getting hurt again. But if he could find the strength to explain how he felt to Holly then maybe they could reach a compromise: she would agree not to pity him *too* much and he'd promise to be content with what they had now and not yearn for what they'd had *then*.

It could work…if Holly really did love him. Did she? Could she? Would she—for ever and always?

He didn't realise he was running until he saw the surprise on Julie's face as he raced past her. He ground to a halt, grinning inanely as he hugged her. 'Thanks!'

'Any time,' she called after him, laughing as she watched him race across the waiting-room and out of the door.

There was a taxi drawing away so he raced after it and banged on the door until the driver stopped then climbed in and told the man to take him to Holly's flat. He had no idea what he was going to say to her but he'd worry about the actual words when he got there. After the mess he'd made of everything over the past two years, there was no point aiming for perfection at this late stage!

CHAPTER TWELVE

HOLLY was slumped in front of the television when the doorbell rang and she sighed as she hauled herself to her feet because it was probably Nicky. It was the third time that week her friend had forgotten her key and Holly had teased her about it the last time, telling her that her absent-mindedness had something to do with Gabriel, and Nicky hadn't denied it.

Was Nicky falling for the handsome new paramedic? Holly wondered as she pressed the button to release the lock on the front door. Probably, and the thought made her feel all churned up inside because it didn't seem fair that other people were falling in love when she was so desperately unhappy.

She opened the front door to the flat then padded back to the sofa and curled up again. She'd put on pyjamas when she'd got home and a pair of fluffy pink bedsocks because she'd still felt chilled from that shower. Maybe she'd caught a cold which would turn to pneumonia, she mused. She'd be admitted to hospital and Ben would come and visit her. And when he saw her lying all pale and wan in the bed then he'd be so overcome that he'd change his mind...

Oh, hell! How *pathetic* could she get?

'Holly?'

Holly yelped when she heard Ben's voice. She

shot off the couch and spun round. He was standing by the door and the expression on his face was something to behold—pain, anguish, joy, hope, regret... She ran through the full list of emotions, mentally ticking them off as they appeared until her head was positively spinning, yet not one of them explained what he was doing there.

'I need to talk to you.'

'What do you want?'

Ben grimaced as he answered her question *before* she'd actually asked it. He took a couple of steps that brought him that bit nearer then stopped when she glared at him.

'Hold it right there,' she ordered in a tone that would have stopped a charging elephant in its tracks. 'I don't know what you're doing here—'

'I need to talk to you,' he repeated with a patience that made her want to throw something at him. Sadly, she only had a cushion to hand and she doubted if it would inflict sufficient damage to make it worth the effort so she glared at him again instead.

'Well, I'm sorry but I'm not interested in anything you have to say. So if you wouldn't mind closing the door behind you as you leave, I'd appreciate it.'

She plonked herself back down on the sofa and turned up the volume on the television so she wouldn't have to hear him going. Tears prickled her eyes but she blinked them away because there was no way she was going to waste any more of her time crying about the wretched man. When a large hand suddenly appeared and gently took the remote control from her, she swung round, more than ready to give him a piece of her mind, but Ben was all ready and prepared.

He tossed the remote control onto the sofa then pulled her up into his arms and kissed her. Holly gasped when she felt his lips plundering hers, groaned when she felt his mouth soften and become so enticing that her bones started melting, kissed him back—albeit with bad grace—when she could no longer resist. She had no idea what was happening in the wider sense but she would worry about that later.

When and *if* she was able.

The kiss went on and on but Ben didn't release her until she was clinging to him. He studied her reddened lips and passion-drugged eyes then nodded. 'That's a start, at least. You've had your pre-op medication so now we can get down to business properly.'

'Properly…'

'Properly,' he repeated in a husky murmur, because his mouth was far too busy finding its way back to hers.

Holly shuddered when she felt the warm, enticing pressure of his lips but, tempting though it was to let him carry on, she had to make him stop. There was just too much at stake to risk making a mistake.

'Ben, stop!' She put her hands on his chest and managed to force an inch-wide gap between them. 'What's this all about? If this is some kind of a game, I really can't handle it.'

'It isn't a game.' He kissed her brow with all the reverence and reserve of a Victorian lover then smiled tenderly at her. 'I love you, Holly. I was an idiot to try and shut you out of my life. I was afraid, you see, and couldn't stand the thought of you pitying me, but I've learned my lesson. If you love me because you pity me then I'll accept it— Oof!'

He doubled over as she gave him a hefty shove in the ribs that forced him to release her. Holly had felt angry on a number of occasions recently but she couldn't recall ever having felt so furious before. She rounded on him, her green eyes spitting fire.

'I don't *pity* you, Ben Carlisle! Why should I when you're making a first-rate job of ladling out all the pity any man could need all by yourself? Yes, I'm sorry you were ill. I'm also scared in case you are ill again in the future, but that's it. *If* I love you— and it's the biggest if in the world at this moment, I have to tell you—then it's because of who you are and not because you've had cancer. Is that clear?'

'I…um…I think so,' he spluttered, looking rather red in the face.

'And as for you being big enough to *accept* my love, well, you should consider yourself lucky that I haven't just told you to get lost!' She put her hands on her hips, mentally gearing herself up for the next round…only it didn't happen the way she'd expected it to. She blinked when she heard the raw apology in his voice.

'I've made a real mess of things again, haven't I? Every time I open my mouth my foot lands in it.' He chuckled and maybe it was the lack of oxygen that made it sound like the sexiest laugh she'd ever heard and maybe not, but Holly felt a tremor run through her.

'You have. At least you're right about something!' she shot back, but even she could tell there wasn't much conviction in her reply. When Ben reached out and pulled her towards him she didn't bother resisting because there was no point. They both knew what was going to happen—she was going back into his arms, he was going to kiss her again and then…

Five minutes was all it took. Holly counted them. One for the kiss. Two to reach her bedroom. Two more to get them both out of their clothes and onto her bed—a record by anyone's standards. She pressed her mouth against Ben's stubbly jaw and grinned. 'I hope you're going to slow down from here on.'

'I can't guarantee it but I do promise to make up for it,' he muttered because his mouth was busy, too.

Holly smiled when she felt his lips nuzzle her left nipple, shuddered when he suckled it, gasped when his mouth travelled down her body so that his tongue could dip delicately into her navel. She wanted to return his caresses, arouse him as much as he was arousing her, but she was already too near the edge to take that risk. Fortunately, so was Ben. One more kiss then he was smiling at her with eyes full of love.

'Will you hate me if I can't hold on any longer?'

'Only if you hate me because I can't either,' she said, biting his shoulder as she guided him inside her.

They made love with a passion that bordered on frenzy so they were both slick with sweat and gasping when it was over. Holly glanced at the bedside clock and chuckled.

'Ten minutes from start to finish, Dr Carlisle. Is that a record?'

'Don't get smart. You're going to regret teasing me,' he threatened, drawing her into his arms and nuzzling her hair. 'I have the rest of the night to prove I can make love to you any way you prefer— fast, slow, medium…'

'All three at once?' she said, laughing at him.

'Or all three at once,' he confirmed deeply. He kissed her softly on the mouth then looked into her eyes. 'I love you so much, Holly. I can't promise you eternity but I can promise you more love than any woman has known before. Is it enough for you to take a chance on me, do you think?'

'It's more than enough.' She kissed him lightly on the mouth, smiled back, loved him with her eyes and her heart and her soul. 'I only ever wanted your love, Ben, and I can cope if it doesn't come with a twenty-year warranty. Yes, I shall worry about you and probably cry the odd tear because I'm only human and I'd like to know that we have for ever and ever. But I'm willing to risk the long term so long as I can have the now, the *this-minute* option. We'll live one day at a time and who knows? All those single days might add up to a whole lifetime in the end. But one thing I do know is that if we don't live them then we'll never find out, will we?'

'And what about children?' His voice roughened because her words had touched him so deeply. 'What if—?'

'There are no *what ifs*. We'll face that problem when the time comes. Not now but then, after we've lived a few more days, one at a time. Together.'

She kissed him gently on the mouth, felt his immediate, rapid response, and it was as though all the fear she'd felt these past few weeks had suddenly ebbed away. They didn't have a guarantee of long life and happiness but that just made what they did have all the more precious. One day at a time, and each one would be filled with their love.

Two years later…

'Have you paged my husband? Where is he? He promised me that he'd be here… Ooh, that hurts!'

Holly gasped as another contraction began. She breathed through it, trying to remember everything she'd learned at her antenatal classes, but it was hard to remember the finer points when she was *in extremis*.

'Where is she? My pager's on the blink and I just got the message…'

'Ben, I'm in here!' Holly called, then groaned as another contraction began. They were coming really close together now but that didn't matter because Ben was here at last. She tried to smile when he came rushing into the delivery suite in a mad panic. 'Don't you dare pass out on me, Dr Carlisle.'

'Would I?' he retorted, grimacing.

He came straight to the bed and knelt down so he could kiss her, his eyes telling her how much he loved her. He'd been thrilled when she'd discovered she was pregnant. It had come out of the blue be-

cause neither of them had expected it to happen after
what he'd been through. However, the consultant had
been very pragmatic when she and Ben had been to
see him for Ben's six-monthly check-up. He'd explained that modern chemotherapy didn't always result in sterility and that Ben's case proved that ad-
mirably. Nevertheless, Holly knew that Ben felt the
same way she did, that this baby was a miracle, and
that made it even more precious. The thought
brought a rush of tears to her eyes and she saw Ben's
expression change to one of alarm.

'Darling, is the pain really bad? Do you want some
gas and air? Or how about some pethidine?'

'Ahem, I'm not sure I appreciate you interfering
with my patient, Dr Carlisle,' the midwife cut in,
winking at Holly over the top of his head.

'I'm sorry but she's in pain!' he protested, looking
so stricken that they both laughed.

Holly lifted his hand to her lips and kissed it. 'I'm
OK, darling. Really. Giving birth *is* painful but the
baby and I are fine— Ooh. Or we will be soon!'

Ben clasped her hand while she rode out the contraction, held it while another one started. They were
on a roll now and Holly concentrated on making sure
she did her bit and in the end it was a textbook delivery. The midwife laid the squalling baby boy on
her tummy while she and Ben just stared in wonder
at the new life they'd created. It *was* a miracle, a seal
on their love and a promise for their future.

Ben laid his hand on his son's wet head and Holly
knew it was another precious memory to add to her
store. She doubted if she would need to break into it

because Ben was so well but it was there to draw on if the time came which, please, God, it never would.

'Thank you, darling. Thank you for giving me so much to look forward to,' he whispered, his hand still touching their child as he bent and kissed her.

Holly kissed him back then laid her hand on top of his. There were three of them now to face the future and it had never seemed brighter.

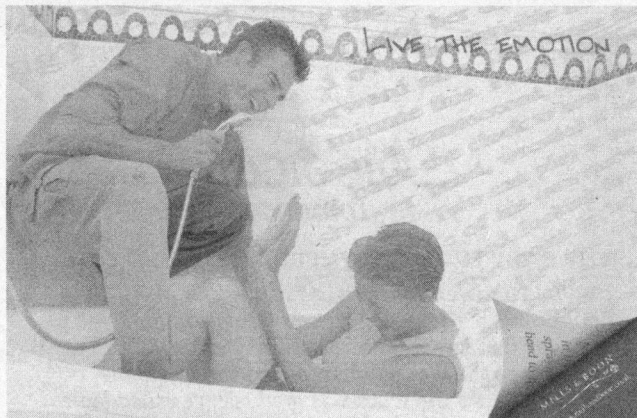

MILLS & BOON®

0804/03b

Live the emotion

Medical
romance™

THE ITALIAN SURGEON'S SECRET
by Margaret Barker

(Roman Hospital)

By leaving England to work in the A&E department of a
Roman hospital Dr Lucy Montgomery hopes to focus
on her career. But with handsome consultant Vittorio
Vincenzi she discovers a bond that soon turns to desire.
Vittorio wants to persuade Lucy to marry him, but he
can't – not yet...

EMERGENCY MARRIAGE *by Olivia Gates*

Dr Laura Burnside was pregnant, single and alone. Her
dream job had been snatched out of her hands by the
arrogant Dr Armando Salazar, and she had nowhere to
go. And then Armando made a proposal that turned her
world upside down: marry him, give her child a father –
and give in to the passion raging between them...

DR CHRISTIE'S BRIDE *by Leah Martyn*

Charming, handsome, a kind and talented doctor –
Jude Christie seems the perfect man. And Dr Kellah
Beaumont finds it impossible to resist when their
growing attraction results in a passionate kiss. But as
she comes to know Jude she realises that he has a
secret standing in the way of their happiness...

On sale 3rd September 2004

*Available at most branches of WHSmith, Tesco, Martins, Borders,
Eason, Sainsbury's and all good paperback bookshops.*

MILLS & BOON®

Volume 3
on sale from
3rd September
2004

Lynne
Graham

International Playboys

*The Desert
Bride*

FREE

4 BOOKS AND A SURPRISE GIFT!

We would like to take this opportunity to thank you for reading this Mills & Boon® book by offering you the chance to take FOUR more specially selected titles from the Medical Romance™ series absolutely FREE! We're also making this offer to introduce you to the benefits of the Reader Service™—

- ★ **FREE home delivery**
- ★ **FREE gifts and competitions**
- ★ **FREE monthly Newsletter**
- ★ **Books available before they're in the shops**
- ★ **Exclusive Reader Service offers**

Accepting these FREE books and gift places you under no obligation to buy; you may cancel at any time, even after receiving your free shipment. Simply complete your details below and return the entire page to the address below. You don't even need a stamp!

YES! Please send me 4 free Medical Romance books and a surprise gift. I understand that unless you hear from me, I will receive 6 superb new titles every month for just £2.69 each, postage and packing free. I am under no obligation to purchase any books and may cancel my subscription at any time. The free books and gift will be mine to keep in any case.

M4ZEE

Ms/Mrs/Miss/Mr...Initials ....
                                                                                            BLOCK CAPITALS PLEASE

Surname ....

Address ....

....

....Postcode ....

Send this whole page to:
The Reader Service, FREEPOST CN81, Croydon, CR9 3WZ

Offer valid in UK only and is not available to current Reader Service™ subscribers to this series. Overseas and Eire please write for details. We reserve the right to refuse an application and applicants must be aged 18 years or over. Only one application per household. Terms and prices subject to change without notice. Offer expires 28th November 2004. As a result of this application, you may receive offers from Harlequin Mills & Boon and other carefully selected companies. If you would prefer not to share in this opportunity please write to The Data Manager at PO Box 676, Richmond, TW9 1WU.

Mills & Boon® is a registered trademark owned by Harlequin Mills & Boon Limited.
Medical Romance™ is being used as a trademark. The Reader Service™ is being used as a trademark.